THE DIARY OF A PARISH CLERK
and other stories

THE DIARY OF A PARISH CLERK
and other stories

Steen Steensen Blicher

Introduction by
Margaret Drabble

Translated by
Paula Hostrup-Jessen

Illustrations by
Povl Christensen

ATHLONE
London & Atlantic Highlands, NJ

First published 1996 by
THE ATHLONE PRESS LTD
1 Park Drive, London NW11 7SG
and 165 First Avenue,
Atlantic Highlands, NJ 07716

© Translation Paula Hostrup-Jessen 1996
© Illustrations The Estate of Povl Christensen 1996

British Library Cataloguing in Publication Data
*A catalogue record for this book is available
from the British Library*

ISBN 0 485 11500 X   hb

Library of Congress Cataloguing-in-Publication Data
Blicher. Steen Steensen, 1782–1848.
    [Short stories. English. Selections]
    The diary of a parish clerk and other stories / Steen Steensen Blicher ; introd. by Margaret Drabble ; translated by Paula Hostrup-Jessen ; illustrations by Povl Christensen.
        p. cm.
    Contents: Blicher's life – The diary of a parish clerk – The gamekeeper at Aunsbjerg – Alas, how changed! – The hosier and his daughter – The Pastor of Vejlbye – Tardy awakening – The three festival eves.
    ISBN 0–485–04851–5 (cloth)
    1. Blicher, Steen Steensen, 1782–1848 – Translations into English. 2. Short stories. Danish – Translations into English. I. Hostrup–Jessen, Paula. II. Christensen, Povl. III. Title.
PT8124.A6   1996
839.8'136–dc20   96-16949
                                                                  CIP

All rights reserved. No part of this publication may be reproduced, stored in a retrieval system, or transmitted in any form or by any means, electronic, mechanical, photocopying or otherwise, without prior permission in writing from the publisher.

Typeset by
Datix International Limited, Bungay, Suffolk

Printed and bound in Great Britain by
Cambridge University Press

Contents

Preface by Erik Harbo — vii
Introduction by Margaret Drabble — ix
Translator's Note — xiv
Steen Steensen Blicher's Life — xv

The Diary of a Parish Clerk — 1
The Gamekeeper at Aunsbjerg — 35
Alas, How Changed! — 57
The Hosier and His Daughter — 81
The Pastor of Vejlbye — 101
Tardy Awakening — 135
Three Festival Eves — 159

Notes — 175
Afterword by Knud Sørensen — 179
Biographical Notes — 187

PREFACE

Denmark's great Golden Age poet and short-story writer, Steen Steensen Blicher, was born curious. And this curiosity aroused in him an interest in Denmark's great neighbour towards the west, even though Britain and Denmark were on opposite sides during the Napoleonic wars. It was initially such Scottish poets as James Macpherson, who appealed to him, and it was the latter's *Poems of Ossian* that subsequently caused him to compare the Scottish Highlands with the Jutland moorland.

Throughout his life Blicher, as pastor, poet, social reformer and hunter, retained his interest in everything British, and continued to find inspiration in British poetry and prose. He asserted in his memoirs that 'More than one Englishman had taken him to be a fellow countryman', despite the fact that English was at that time only spoken in Denmark by sailors and merchants. Famous novelists like Goldsmith and Scott were normally read in Danish translation.

This Scottish/English inspiration has given the Blicher Society reason to believe that there is a basis for sending this present selection, consisting of seven out of the available ninety short stories, across the North Sea, and outwards to the English-speaking world at large.

During his lifetime many of Blicher's stories were translated into German, and it would have pleased him to know that they have also been published in English. The aging writer's last application to the Danish king was for funds for a journey to Westmoreland in order to study the links between the English language and the Jutland dialect, and visit his friend, the linguist Richard Cleasby. But this journey never came about. When, in 1847, Cleasby died, Blicher wrote in a poem in

English: 'Yes, I have had you in my house/ and in my church, where you stood listening/ with awe and sung our Danish hymns.' Shortly afterwards Blicher himself died, leaving his short stories, which, together with Hans Christian Andersen's fairy tales, are among the greatest of Danish nineteenth-century literature.

The Blicher Society is delighted that this edition has come into being, and wishes to thank everyone, from the translator Paula Hostrup-Jessen, the authors Margaret Drabble and Knud Sørensen, the consultant, Professor Sven H. Rossel, Seattle, to the many Blicher devotees who have supported this venture in other ways.

The Society also wishes to thank The Athlone Press for their co-operation, as well as Queen Margrethe II and H.R.H. Prince Henrik's Foundation, Oskar and Lida Nielsen's Foundation, Konsul Georg Jorck and Emma Jorck's Foundation, The Danish Ministry for Foreign Affairs, The Royal Danish Embassy in London and The Danish Literary Information Centre for their economic support.

Erik Harbo
Chairman of the Blicher Society

INTRODUCTION

Margaret Drabble

Steen Steensen Blicher is a writer whose work, although proudly and profoundly Danish in character, was much influenced by English and Scottish literature. He never came to Britain – indeed most of his life was spent in his native Jutland – but his stories reveal strong links with our own literary history. Yet their interest is not antiquarian. They are as lively and accessible today as when they were first published.

Blicher speaks to us with apparent directness, arresting the reader's attention with an informal tone of personal intimacy and immediacy. His matter and manner seem engagingly simple: one can well understand why in Denmark he remains a classic, popular with readers of all ages. But on closer inspection, or on a second reading, we become aware that his stories work on several levels, and are neither as artless nor as naive as they appear. The short story as a form was young in his hands, when he published his first prose piece in 1824, and he developed it with a masterly narrative skill. He speaks to us, in fact, in many voices, all carefully differentiated. He prefers the first person, but we cannot trust what this first person tells us, for Blicher introduces us to a variety of what are now recognised as 'unreliable narrators', and many of the stories serve also as dramatic monologues, unfolding to us the personality, the prejudices, and the limitations of the story teller, as well as events of the tale he tells.

We meet here, in these freshly-translated versions, the parish clerk, perhaps Blicher's most celebrated character study, whose life remorselessly unfolds from the high hopes of youth to tragic stoicism; the child Steen, learning of but not quite comprehending adult passion and sacrifice; the poetic fop boasting of Copenhagen fashions, teased and mocked by the village maiden; the wandering scholar, accidental witness to a tale of violence and derangement; the anguished judge, presiding helplessly over a mystifying miscarriage of justice; and the pastor, unable to give comfort to his closest friend. In each story of this collection (except the last, 'The Three Festival Eves', which represents a slightly different folk mode) we are aware of a psychological complexity beyond the immediate grasp of those who act as recorders or participants: Blicher, with remarkable economy, suggests an unexplored hinterland of suffering and longing. His style is lucid, but his characters elude simple moral judgements.

Perhaps the most enigmatic of his figures is 'Mrs L', the anti-heroine of 'Tardy Awakening', an intriguing precursor of Flaubert's Madame Bovary, or of some of Kipling's frustrated wives on the British Raj. The actions of this seductive small-town beauty are open to many interpretations: both her sexual desires and her calm acceptance of them are utterly convincing yet strangely opaque. She is a startling creation for a Jutland pastor, and we certainly cannot identify the pastor who describes her with the pastor Blicher who created both narrator and unfaithful wife. Scandalous stories were told about Blicher's own wife, and one feels there may be some autobiographical feeling here, but there is no edge of resentment. He writes neither as sentimentalist nor as satirist.

Beyond Blicher's psychological realism lies another hinterland. In the natural world which inspired both his prose and his poetry. His work is a powerful evocation of the Jutland landscape, with its bogs and brown moorland, its skylarks, its vipers, its stags, grouse and bittern, and its scattered population of peasants, farmers, poachers, gypsies, and huntsmen. A keen huntsman himself, Blicher uses many metaphors drawn from the sport, and his description of the duck-shoot in 'Alas! How Changed' is a small comic masterpiece. Writing in the Golden Age of Danish romanticism, he embodies the Romantic faith shared by his British and German contemporaries: he believed that we are formed by the landscape we inhabit.

Yet this landscape too has its paradoxes. Is it eternal, or is it in itself a symbol of change and decay? Blicher, like Walter

Scott, whom he greatly admired (though he did not like to be described as his imitator), was keenly aware that country ways of life, in the nineteenth century, were subject to irreversible change, and, like Scott, he was anxious to record them before they vanished, and to stimulate, if possible, a pride that would keep some of them alive. The theme of the passage of time sounds as a constant threnody in his prose, and it is no accident that his first published works were translations of the *Poems of Ossian*, by the Scottish poet James Macpherson. Ossian was said to be the last of his race, the last of the Gaelic bards of a vanished Scotland, and Blicher at times clearly saw himself as an isolated voice speaking from a remote world: Ossian's Scotland becomes Blicher's Jutland.

Did Blicher represent an end or a beginning? Like Scott himself, he represented both. Scott loved to dwell on heroic defeat, on the lay of the last minstrel, on the death of the Highlands, yet he created the historical novel as we know it – indeed, it is not too much to say that he helped to create the image of Scotland as we know it. Similarly Blicher, although possessed of a profound melancholy, a deep sense of the futility of human endeavour, and an interest in and sympathy with loss of class and status, was an energetic innovator. He opened the eyes of Denmark to the rugged beauties of one of its apparently less-favoured regions: he created the sensibility which would appreciate and conserve it. It is no surprise to discover that his work is invoked by the Danish Tourist Board.

Romanticism, as a movement, looked both ways, to the past and to the future. Its early stirrings, in the late eighteenth century, were more marked by a nostalgic sense of loss than by a revolutionary fervour: Ossian was only one of the 'end of the race' figures who attracted literary attention. Goldsmith wrote about the deserted village and the 'last and greatest' of the Irish bards, the blind Carolan; William Cowper wrote about lone castaways and blasted oaks and fallen avenues, and was quoted with approval by the anti-romantic Jane Austen. Thomas Gray, in 'The Bard', celebrated the last poet of Wales, defeated and forced to suicide by the invading English army under Edward I. A few decades later, Byron saw himself as 'the last and youngest of a noble line' ('Elegy on Newstead Abbey'), Southey sang of the 'Last of the Goths', and Mary Shelley in 1826 published a novel about the end of the world called *The Last Man*. One can see links of mood and subject in all these authors, most of whom blended a sense of patriotism with an awareness of inevitable defeat.

We can also see a connection with Walter Scott's exact contemporary, William Wordsworth. Wordsworth, like Blicher, was a man whose writing sprang from deep roots in place: like Blicher, he chose to wander the countryside, alone and on foot, interesting himself in all conditions of people. He met and cross-questioned shepherds, farmers, gypsies, tinkers, and women driven mad by loss. A character like the Hosier's Daughter would not be out of place in Wordsworth's first volume, *Lyrical Ballads*, and Blicher would, one feels, have recognised the dignity of Wordsworth's Simon Lee the Huntsman. Both writers sought the company of ordinary, often inarticulate people: indeed, Blicher extended his researches further than Wordsworth, for he is said in later years to have been quite at home drinking in the canal-side taverns of low-life Copenhagen, and unlike Wordsworth, although he became famous, he never became thoroughly respectable.

There is something poignant about the figure of Steen Steensen Blicher, Denmark's most celebrated author, shabby, in debt, and given to drink, wandering the countryside like a Wordsworthian beggar, like the ghost of himself. Yet this forlorn and seemingly helpless victim was and remained a highly conscious artist, keenly aware of the aesthetic and technical problems of presenting a world as yet unpainted and unsung. In his work, he was no primitive. Should he, we can see and hear him wonder, opt for a 'Scottish realism' of overloaded detail, or for the discursive style of the village storyteller, or for the detached scholarly narrator, or for mock-epic, or for a Netherlandish 'low-life' canvas? His varied choices are all deliberate. He may well have learned not only from Scott and Ossian, but also from the innocent first-person tale of Goldsmith's long-suffering and heartbreakingly optimistic Vicar of

Wakefield, whose adventures Blicher also translated. Yet Blicher's style and his subjects are his own, and they are timeless.

In one of his finest works, 'The Diary of a Parish Clerk', through one voice recording one bewildered and disappointed life, Blicher can make us hear the sound of history. Morten Vinge, in his last diary entry, describes himself as 'a leafless tree on the moors' and 'the last of my family': the phrases have a romantic, Ossianic ring, but Morten and Blicher have outlived Ossian, and they share a stubborn brave resilience. Macpherson's Ossian was a sentimental forgery: Blicher's Morten is the real thing.

TRANSLATOR'S NOTE

FOOTNOTES

Since Steen Steensen Blicher himself employed footnotes, not only in order to clarify various terms and phrases in the Jutland dialect but also to provide dramatic effect, I have retained those of his footnotes which are relevant to the English translation. They are to be found at the foot of the page concerned. Additional notes which I have considered helpful for the English-speaking reader are collected page by page at the end of the book.

I should like to thank Professor Sven H. Rossel of the University of Washington, who has acted as consultant on this project, the opera singer Erik Harbo, Chairman of the Blicher Society, for his help with the Jutland dialect and Blicher's characteristic use of the Danish language, and, not least, my husband Carl Hostrup for his never-failing support.

I am grateful to the Danish Literary Information Centre for financial support, and to the British Centre for Literary Translation, University of East Anglia, for providing me with a month's respite from other tasks. I am furthermore indebted to the social historian, Dr Victor Morgan of the University of East Anglia, who helped to clear up several trans-cultural translation problems.

Paula Hostrup-Jessen

STEEN STEENSEN BLICHER'S LIFE

1782   Blicher is born in Vium parsonage on 11 October.
1796   The family moves to Randlev in East Jutland.
1796   Pupil at Randers grammar school.
1799   Matriculation. Commences theological studies at the University of Copenhagen.
1807   Publishes Vol. I of the translation of *Poems of Ossian*.
1809   Publishes Vol. II.
1809   Obtains a doctorate in theology.
1810   Appointed master at Randers grammar school. Marries his late uncle's 17-year-old widow, Ernestine Juliane.
1811   Appointed farm manager at father's parsonage in Randlev.
1814   Publishes first collection of poetry, *Poems. Part I*.
1819   Appointed pastor of Thorning-Lysgaard.
1824   Publishes his first short story, *Fragments from the Diary of a Parish Clerk*.
1826   Appointed pastor of Spentrup-Gassum.
1827   Publishes translation of Oliver Goldschmidt's *The Vicar of Wakefield*.
1828   Writes his first poem in the Jutland dialect, inspired by the Scottish poet William Laidlaw.
1833   Publishes his short stories for the first time in book form.
1839   Arranges the first big mass meeting in Denmark on the Jutland hill, "Himmelbjerg" (Sky-Mountain).
1842   Collects his dialectal writings and publishes the work, *E Bindstouw* (The Knitting-Room), with its genuine appeal to the common people.
1848   Dies on 26 March.

Blicher wrote 95 short stories and about 340 poems. He is the author of several translations and wrote many works dealing with rural economy and social reform. His complete oeuvre fills 33 volumes, *c.* 7000 printed pages.

THE DIARY OF A PARISH CLERK

Føulum, January 1st, 1708

God grant us all a happy New Year, and save our good Pastor Søren! He snuffed out the candle last night, and mother says he will not live to see the next New Year[1] – but I dare say this has no significance. It was nonetheless an enjoyable evening: when Pastor Søren took off his cap after supper and said, in his usual fashion, *'agamus gratias!'*[2], he pointed at me instead of Jens. This was the first time I had read our Latin grace. A year ago today Jens said it; but then I had listened wide-eyed, for I didn't understand a word, and now I know half of Cornelius[3]. I have a feeling I shall become the Pastor of Føulum. Oh, how happy my dear parents would be should they live to

see that day! And then the pastor's Jens could become the
Bishop of Viborg – as his father says. Well, who can tell? Everything is in the hands of God. His will be done! *Amen in nomine
Jesu!*[4]

Føulum, September 3rd, 1708

Yesterday, by the grace of God, I completed my fifteenth year.
Jens cannot rival me in Latin now. I am more diligent than he
is: I stay at home and study, while he goes out hunting with
Peer the gamekeeper. He will never become a bishop like that.
Poor Pastor Søren! He knows it, to be sure; his eyes fill with
tears when he sometimes says to him, '*mi fili! mi fili! otium est
pulvinar diaboli!*'[5]

At New Year we are to start Greek. Pastor Søren has given
me a Testament in Greek. 'It's a strange kind of scrawl, don't
you think? And it still completely baffles you,' he said kindly,
pinching my ear, as he always does when he is in a good
mood. But bless us! – how surprised he will be when he hears I
can read quite fast already!

Føulum, die St. Martini[6]

Jens is heading for a fall. Pastor Søren was so vexed with him
that he spoke Danish to him all day. To me he spoke Latin;
once I heard him say, as if to himself: '*vellem hunc esse filium
meum!*'[7] It was me he meant. And how miserably Jens stammered at his Cicero! I know very well how it came about,
because the day before yesterday, while his father was at a
wedding in Vinge, he was with Peer the gamekeeper over
in Lindum woods, and – God save us! – a wild boar tore his
breeches to shreds. He lied to his mother and said that the
Thiele bull had done it; but she boxed his ears soundly –
habeat![8]

Føulum, Calendis Januar[9], 1709

Proh dolor! Pastor Søren is dead – *vae me miserum!*[10] When we
had sat down to dinner on Christmas Eve, he put down his

spoon and looked long and sorrowfully at Jens – *'fregisti cor meum,'*[11] he sighed, and went into his bedchamber. Alas, he never rose from his bed again. Since then I have visited him every day, and he has given me much instruction and good counsel; but now I shall never see him again. On Thursday I saw him for the last time; never shall I forget what he said after he had spoken to me most movingly: 'God give my son an upright heart!' He folded his bony hands and sank back on the pillow: *'pater! in manus tuas committo spiritum meum!'*[12] Those were his last words. When I saw the pastor's wife put her apron to her eyes, I ran out feeling very ill at ease. Jens was standing outside the door weeping. *'Seras dat poenas turpi poenitentia,'*[13] I thought; but he fell on my neck and sobbed. God forgive him his wildness! That is what has grieved me the most.

Føulum, Pridie iduum Januarii MDCCIX.[14]

Yesterday my dear father went to Viborg to arrange for my dinners when I start school. How I long for that time! I study all day, to be sure, but the days are so short now, and mother says we cannot afford candles to read by. I cannot make head or tail of that letter to Tuticanus[15] – no, things were very different when good Pastor Søren was alive. *Eheu! Mortuus est!*[16]

It is a terrible winter! The snowstorm wages furiously; there is a snowdrift reaching right to the ridge of our barn. Last night Jens shot two hares in our kitchen garden – he will soon have forgotten his poor father. But if Peer the gamekeeper finds out there will be trouble.

Føulum, Idibus Januarii[17], MDCCIX

Father has not come home yet, and the weather is as foul as ever – if only he doesn't lose his way. There goes Jens up at the barn, with his gun and a brace of birds in his hand – he's coming in here . . .

They were partridges he had shot on Mads Madsen's dunghill. He wanted mother to roast them, but she didn't dare, for the gentry might come to hear of it!

Føulum, XVIII Calend. Febr.[18]

Alas, alas! My dear father has frozen to death! The Squire of Kokholm found him in a snowdrift and has brought him home in his cart. I have wept so much that I can scarcely see out of my eyes – my mother as well. God help us both!

Føulum, February 18th

I hardly recognized Jens again – in the green coat he was wearing, and with a green feather in his cap. 'Can't you see', he said, 'I'm a huntsman now! And what are you? A schoolboy, a Latin-babbler!' 'Nay, God help us!' I replied, 'my Latin days are over. I can be the pastor where you're the bishop! My mother shall not starve to death while I'm singing at people's doors in Viborg.[19] I must stay at home and earn her keep. Alas, Jens, if only your father had lived!' 'Don't let's talk about that!' he said. 'I should never in my life have learnt Latin – the Devil take such twaddle! Now, listen! – you could get a place up at the Manor. You'd have a good time and live well!' 'How should I manage that?' I replied. 'Well, we'll have a try!' he shouted, and ran off. After all, he is good-natured, is Jens, but wild and untamed. Six weeks ago they buried his poor father and three weeks ago his mother followed him. But now he appears quite unconcerned. He can cry one moment and laugh the next.

Thiele, May 1st, 1709

So now I'm a servant in his lordship's household! Farewell parsonage! Farewell Latin! Oh, my precious books! *valete plurimum! vendidi libertatem*[20] for 8 rix-dollars. Eight of those my poor mother must have, and his lordship has promised her wood from the forest besides, so she will neither starve nor freeze. It is really Jens who has found me this place. He has great influence here at the manor; he's the devil of a fellow – a ladies' man! The housekeeper gave him a big piece of cake, the dairymaid smirked kindly at him, the chambermaid likewise, and even one of the young ladies nodded at him in a friendly way as she passed by. It seems as if he may become the gamekeeper in place of Peer. The worst of it is that he has got into the habit of swearing worse than any sailor.

Thiele, May 12th, 1709

I am getting on quite well, God be praised! We are six servants to wait upon the master, the mistress, the young gentleman and the two young ladies. I have time enough to read, and I do not neglect my beloved books. They may not be of any use to me, but I cannot stop doing so nevertheless. Yesterday the late Pastor Søren's books were sold. I spent two rix-dollars, and got as many as I could carry – among them many volumes of Ovid. One is entitled *'ars amoris'*, another *'remedium amoris'*[21]; these I shall read first, for I am curious to learn what they are about. Once I chanced upon them in Pastor Søren's study, but he came and snatched them away from me, saying, *'abstine manus!* Hands off! That's nothing for you!'

Thiele, June 3rd, 1709

If only I understood French! The family speak little else at table, and I cannot understand a word. Today they were talking about me, for they kept on looking at me. Once I nearly dropped the plate; I was standing behind Miss Sophie's chair, when she turned round and looked me straight in the face. She is a beautiful young lady, Miss Sophie[22] – a joy to behold.

Thiele, September 13th, 1709

Yesterday was quite a busy day. The people from Viskum were here, and there was a big hunt. I took part as well, and was handed one of his lordship's guns. At first all went well, but then a wolf came running past me. I nearly dropped the gun from sheer fright, and quite forgot to shoot. Jens was standing beside me and shot at the wolf. 'You're a blockhead!' he cried, 'but I won't give you away.' Shortly afterwards his lordship went past. 'You're a dolt, *Martin*!' he cried. 'You accept bribes!'[23] 'I most humbly beg your forgiveness, my Lord!' I replied. 'I am quite innocent, but someone must have been speaking ill of me. I shall, God willing, serve you honestly and faithfully, my Lord!' At this he laughed benevolently, and repeated, 'You're a great dolt!' But that was not the end of it:

when the gentry were seated at table they started speaking about the wolf again, and asked me how much he paid me, and so forth. I don't quite know what they meant, but this much I did understand: they were making fun of me both in French and Danish. And even Miss Sophie was laughing at me to my face – that hurt me most of all. Surely I should be able to learn that nasal tongue? It could scarcely be more difficult than Latin!

Thiele, October 2nd, 1709

It is not impossible – that I can see. French is nothing else but bad Latin. In among a case of old books I had bought there was also a *Metamorphoses* in French – it came in capitally! I already understood it in Latin. But one thing is odd: when I hear them talking upstairs, I don't seem to hear any French words – they are certainly not discussing Ovid.

I must also set about learning to shoot. His lordship likes me to go hunting with him, but at such times I can never do anything to please him: either he scolds or else he laughs at me – sometimes both at once. I carry the gun in the wrong way, I load it in the wrong way, I take aim in the wrong way and I shoot in the wrong way. I must ask Jens to teach me. 'Look at Jens!' says his lordship. 'There's a huntsman for you! You carry your gun as if it were a scythe slung over your shoulder, and when you take aim it looks as if you are about to fall over backwards.' Miss Sophie laughs at me too; it suits her nevertheless – she has such beautiful teeth.

Thiele, November 7th, 1709

Yesterday I shot a fox; his lordship called me a stout *garçon* and gave me an inlaid powder horn as a present. Jens's instruction has borne fruit. This shooting is quite good fun.

My French is getting better now. I am beginning to get hold of the pronunciation. The other day I listened at the door while Mademoiselle was teaching the young ladies. When they had finished and gone upstairs I stole in to see what book they might be using. Good gracious! How amazed I was! It was the very same book as the one I have, which is called: *'L'École du Monde.'*[24] Now I listen outside the door every day with book in hand – that works very well. The French tongue is much more beautiful than I thought; Miss Sophie looks so charming when she speaks it.

Thiele, December 13th, 1709

Yesterday, with God's help, I saved his lordship's life. We held a *battue* in Lindum woods. Just as we reached Graakjaer a wild boar emerges and makes straight for his lordship. He shot and hit it, to be sure, but that wasn't sufficient, and the wild boar goes for him. His lordship was not afraid: he draws his hunting-knife and is about to plunge it into the boar's breast – but it breaks in two. This was a fine state of affairs – it all happened so quickly that no one could come to his aid. Just as I am making for the spot I see his lordship on the back of the boar, which is making off with him. 'Shoot!' he shouts at the bailiff, who was stationed to the left of him; but he was afraid. 'Shoot, in the Devil's name!' he shouts at Jens, as he charges past him; Jens's gun misfired. Then the boar turned and rushed straight past me. 'Shoot, Morten, or the boar will ride to Hell with me!' he screamed. In God's name, I thought, took aim at the animal's hindquarters and was fortunate enough to smash both of its legs. How happy I was, and so were we all, but most of all his lordship. 'That was a masterly shot', he said, 'you may keep the gun you have put to such good use! And listen to me, you womanish oaf!' he said to the bailiff. 'Mark the biggest beech in the forest for Morten's old mother! Jens can go home and put a better flint in his gun!' When we came home in the evening there were many questions and many tales to tell. His lordship patted me on the back, and Miss Sophie smiled at me so kindly that my heart was in my mouth.

Thiele, January 11th, 1710

Pleasant weather! The sun rises as red as a burning ember! It looks quite remarkable, shining through the white trees like that; all the trees look as if they were powdered, and their branches hang around them, brushing the ground. The old Grand Richard[25] is in peril – two of its branches have already snapped. The weather was precisely the same a week ago when we drove to Fussingøe and I stood on the runners of Miss Sophie's sledge. She herself wished to take the reins, but after a quarter of an hour had passed her small fingers began to freeze. *'J'ai froid,'*[26] she murmured. 'Would you like me to drive, Miss?' I asked. *'Comment!'*[27] she said. 'Do you understand French?' *'Un peu, mademoiselle,'*[28] I replied. Then she turned and looked me full in the face. I took one of the reins in each hand and had both my arms around her. I held them wide apart in order to keep my distance, but every time the sledge gave a jolt and I came to touch her it was as if I touched a raging furnace. It felt as if I were flying through the air with her, and before I knew it we were in Fussingøe. If she had not called out, *'Tenez, Martin! arrestez-vous!'*[29] I would have driven straight on to Randers or even to the end of the world. I wonder if she would like to go for a ride again today? But here

comes Jens with his lordship's gun, which he has been cleaning – so we are going out hunting.

Thiele, February 13th, 1710

I don't feel very well. It's as if a heavy stone were lying on my breast. I have no appetite, and at night I cannot sleep. Last night I had a strange dream; it was as if I were standing on the runners of Miss Sophie's sledge, but all at once I was sitting inside the sledge with her on my lap. I had my right arm around her waist, and she her left arm around my neck. She bent down and kissed me, but in the same instant I woke up. Alas, if only I could have gone on dreaming! It was a fine book, the one she lent me; I divert myself with it every evening – if only one could be as happy as that Tartar prince![30] The more French I read, the better I like it; it is almost making me forget my Latin.

Thiele, March 13th, 1710

Yesterday, when we returned from shooting snipe, his lordship said to me: 'I hear that you understand French?' 'A little, sir,' I replied. 'Then you cannot very well wait at table; we shouldn't be able to open our mouths with you there.' 'Oh', I cried, 'your lordship surely won't send me away?' '*Point de tout*,'[31] he replied. 'From now on you shall be my *valet-de-chambre*![32] And when Master Kresten leaves for Paris, you shall accompany him – what do you say to that?' I was so moved that I couldn't say a word, but kissed his hand. But although I look forward to it so much, I dread the thought of leaving, and since then I really believe that my health has worsened.

Thiele, May 1st 1710

Alas, unhappy man that I am! Now I know what is troubling me: Ovid has enlightened me – he has accurately described my illness. If I am not mistaken it is called *Amor*, or love, and she who has captivated me must beyond all doubt be Miss Sophie. Oh, what a poor fool I am! What will be the end of it? I must try his *remedia amoris*!

Just now I saw her standing in the passage talking in a friendly manner to Jens – it was like a knife in my heart. I could have put a bullet through his head; but then she skipped past me with a smile. It felt like when I'm out hunting and the quarry comes within range of my gun: my heart pounds against my ribs, I can scarcely breathe and my eyes are as if riveted to the animal – *ah, malheureux que je suis!*[33]

Thiele, June 17th, 1710

Oh, how empty and wearisome the manor seems now. The gentry are away and won't be back for eight whole days. However shall I get through them? I don't feel like doing anything at all. My gun is hanging there, dirty and rusty, and I can't be bothered to clean it. I don't understand how Jens and the others can be so merry and bright: the yard echoes with their chatter and laughter, while I sigh like a bittern. Alas, Miss Sophie! If you were but a peasant girl and I a prince!

Thiele, June 28th, 1710

Today the manor seems as if it were newly white-washed and decorated. The trees in the garden have taken on a beautiful shade of pale green and everyone looks so contented. Miss Sophie has come home again: she came in through the gate like the sun bursting through a cloud, and yet I trembled like an aspen leaf. Being in love is both good and bad.

Thiele, October 4th, 1710

What a magnificent hunt we had today! Hvidding Copse was surrounded by over three hundred beaters; for they had come from both Viskum and Fussingøe with all their hounds. We from Thiele had been there since daybreak. There was hardly a breath of wind, and a heavy mist covered the entire neighbourhood; only the tops of the beacons were visible above. Far away we could hear the heavy footsteps of the beaters and the occasional baying of a hound. 'They are coming from Viskum now', said his lordship, 'I can hear Chasseur's bark.' 'They are coming from Fussingøe too', said Jens, 'that is Perdrix baying.' We could still not see anything through the mist, but as they drew nearer we heard the rumble of the carts, the snorting of the horses and the chatter and laughter of the huntsmen. Then the sun broke through and the mist lifted; soon it was bustling with activity on all sides. The gamekeepers were already beginning to post the beaters – we could hear them whispering and hushing up those who talked too loudly – and sometimes their staves went into action. The huntsmen came riding from the west and the south, and behind them the carts with the hounds; their tails wagged over the sides of the carts, and sometimes a head protruded – only to get a box on the ear from the huntsmen's boys. Then his lordship himself posted the huntsmen down along the valley that runs through the middle of the copse. When he had finished he blew his whistle, and the horn-blowers at once began to play a merry tune. The hounds were set loose, and it was not long before they started baying – first one, then two, then the whole pack. Hares, foxes and deer darted back and forth among the tree-covered hills. Now and then a shot rang out, and the reports echoed down through the valley. We could not see the beaters, but could hear their shouts and cries when a deer or a hare tried to break through the cordon. I held my post and shot two foxes and a buck before breakfast. While we were eating the hounds were called together and tied up and the horn-blowers played, and when that was over the fun started again. See! Just then two carriages drew up at the end of the valley with all the ladies, among them Miss Sophie. That saved a fox; while I was looking over there, he slipped right past me. A couple of hours before nightfall the copse was cleared of game and the hunt came to an end. We had shot close on thirty animals, and Master Kresten, who had shot the most foxes, was celebrated with a tune on the horn.

Thiele, December 17th, 1710

Yesterday I followed my dear mother to her last resting-place. The new pastor – may God reward him! – honoured her passing with a funeral sermon that lasted an hour and three quarters. She was a good and kind mother to me – God grant her a blessed resurrection!

Thiele, January 23rd, 1711

A miserable winter! No sledging yet! I have been longing for that ever since Martinmas, but in vain. Rain and storm, southerly winds and dreary weather. It was this time last year that we drove to Fussingøe – how I dream of that night! The moon shone as bright as a silver platter in the blue sky, casting our shadows up on the white snow by the roadside. Now and again I leant over so that my shadow merged with Miss Sophie's – then it felt as if we two were one. We had a cold wind right in our faces; it blew her sweet breath back to me, and I drank it like wine. Oh, what a fool, what a lovesick fool I am! What is the use of all these deliberations? On Sunday I am leaving for Copenhagen with Master Kresten, and we are to remain there all summer. I think I shall be dead before Mayday. Ah, Mademoiselle Sophie. Adieu! un éternel adieu![34]

At sea between Samsø and Zealand, February 3rd, 1711

The sun is setting behind my beloved Jutland; its reflection stretches over the calm waters like an endless path of flame. It seems to bear a greeting from my home. Alas! it is far away, and I am leaving it farther and farther behind. I wonder what they are doing at Thiele now? My right ear is burning – I wonder if Miss Sophie might be talking about me? Alas, no! I am only a poor servant, after all – why should she think of me? Just as little as the skipper, who paces to and fro on the deck with folded arms. He glances so frequently towards the north – I wonder what there is to see? 'A Swede,' he says. God help us in His mercy and goodness!

Kallundborg, Feb 4th, 1711

Now I know all about war[35] – I have been in battle, and – the Lord of Sabaoth be praised! – victory was ours. The skipper was right – it was a Swedish privateer. This morning, at first light, we saw him about two miles away; the crew said he was chasing us. 'Are there any of you passengers', said the skipper, 'who have pluck and stout hearts, and a wish to tussle with that Swedish fellow?' 'I have a good rifle', replied Master Kresten, 'and my servant has one too. Shall we not have a go at it, Morten?' 'As you please, young master!' I said, and ran down into the cabin, loaded our rifles and brought them up on deck together with powder and shot. Two soldiers from Jutland had come up from the hold, each with his musket, the skipper had a Spanish rifle as long as he was tall, while the first mate and the seamen came with axes and handspikes. 'Couldn't we simply make off, good captain?' I asked. 'The Devil we could,' he replied. 'Can't you see he's gaining on us as fast as he can? You will soon be able to hear his cannon. But if you're afraid, you can go home and hide in your mother's old chest.' Just as he spoke, smoke poured out of the Swedish vessel, and immediately afterwards we heard a terrible noise and the sound of something whizzing over our heads. Before long there was another report, and yet another, and finally a cannon-ball tore a splinter from our mast. That made me feel strangely ill at ease: my heart began to pound and my ears to buzz. But when the Swede came close enough to be within range of our rifles and I had taken my first shot, I began to feel as if I were on a *battue*. The Swede came closer and closer, and we stood under cover of the cabin, firing across our stern at him for all we were worth. Several of his men fell, most of them hit by the young master and me. 'If we can shoot a snipe, Morten, we can surely hit a Swede when he's standing still!' he said. 'Brave lads!' shouted the skipper. 'Can you see the Swedish captain – the man pacing up and down with the big sword? If you can pick him off, then the game is ours!' So I took aim at him, pulled the trigger, and as I lowered my rifle I saw him hit the deck. 'Hurrah!' shouted the skipper together with the rest of us; but the privateer turned about and made off. With the Danish flag aloft we sailed into Kallundborg Fjord, very proud and very happy, for not one of us was wounded, although the bullets had flown over and through the ship. Monsieur Hartman, the tutor, was the only one to spill any blood, and that in a singular fashion. He was lying smoking his pipe in the skipper's bunk when the fight began. Shortly afterwards I went down to fetch some tow for the bullets. *'Martine!'* he said, *'quid hoc sibi vult?'*[36] But before I could answer, a bullet flew straight through the porthole, carrying off his pipe, which was sticking out over the edge of the bunk, and the mouthpiece tore a gash in the roof of his mouth.

Now we are in the harbour and on dry land, where rest is sweet after such a bout!

Copenhagen, June 2nd, 1711

My head is quite full of all the strange things I have seen and heard. I cannot collect my thoughts, for one chases away the next like clouds before the wind. But the strangest thing of all is that I am almost cured of my lovesickness. The longer I stay here, the less I seem to pine for Miss Sophie, and I am almost ready to believe there are just as beautiful girls in Copenhagen. If I were to write a footnote to *Ovidii remedium amoris*, I would recommend a visit to the capital as one of the best remedies for that dangerous malady.

At anchor off Kronborg, September 12th, 1711

Oh, gracious Heaven! What have I not witnessed! What misery and wretchedness have I not seen with my own eyes! God has punished us for our sins and stricken the people with blains.[37] They were dying like flies around me, but I, unworthy that I am, was delivered from the jaws of death. Alas, my dear young master! What shall I say when I return without him? But I did not forsake him till he had drawn his last breath; I risked my life for him, and yet God spared it – praised be His name! When I think of those horrifying days my heart is ready to break. Silent and afraid, we sat from morning till night in our lonely chambers, looking at each other and sighing. We glanced only rarely down into the deserted streets; where previously they had been swarming with people, only an occasional *triste figure* would glide ghost-like over the cobbles. But through the windows you could see people sitting like prisoners, most of them motionless – as if they had been painted portraits. On hearing the hollow rumbling of the death-carts, they would all rush away from the windows in order not to witness the dreadful sight! I saw it only once, and never wish to see it again. There they were – the black angels of death, driving their long carts full of corpses, which were piled up on one another like cattle. Out of the back of the cart hung the head and arms of a young woman, the eyes staring horribly in the blackened yellow face and the long hair sweeping the street. Then for the first time my young master was really upset; he tottered into his bedchamber and lay down on his death-bed, while deep in my heart I sighed: 'Like sheep they are laid in the grave; death shall feed on them, but God will redeem my soul from the power of the grave: for He shall receive me. Selah!'

Thiele, September 29th, 1711

So now I am here again. As I entered the gate my heart pounded almost as strongly as on the day we fought the Swede. And when I entered the room and saw his lordship and all his family dressed in black I wept like a child, and they wept too. I could scarcely speak for tears, and before I had come to the end of that dreadful story, his lordship turned aside and went into his bedchamber – God comfort them in His mercy, Amen!

Thiele, October 8th, 1711

Today was the first time we have been out hunting since my homecoming. Alas, it was not like former times, and gave but little satisfaction. 'Morten', his lordship repeated again and again, 'how we miss Master Kresten!' – and he sighed fit to break my heart. We came home long before nightfall with one puny hare.

Thiele, Nov. 2nd, 1711

The house is coming to life again; we expect very distinguished visitors: His Excellency, Lord Gyldenløve with his train.[38] He is to stay here for a few weeks and divert himself with the chase. Yesterday the gentry talked about it at table. 'He is of royal blood and a perfect gentleman,' said her ladyship, glancing across at Miss Sophie. She blushed, looked down at her plate and smiled, but I became as cold as ice all over. Alas, I thought I was cured of my foolish infatuation, but I can feel the malady has returned with even greater force. I struggle like a partridge in a net, but to no avail – if only I were a thousand miles from here!

Thiele, Nov. 14th, 1711

His Excellency has arrived at last, and with the greatest imaginable pomp and circumstance: two footmen with tall hats trimmed with silver came running into the courtyard half a mile ahead. They posted themselves with their long gaily coloured staves on either side of the great door. Her ladyship wriggled in at one door and out of the other; never before have I seen her so agile. Miss Sophie stood in the best parlour, gazing alternatively at the mirror and out of the window. She didn't notice me at all when I passed through the room. At last he himself drove up in a carriage drawn by six yellow horses – a handsome, fine-looking gentleman. He looked both distinguished and gracious, and yet I felt there was something repulsive about him. His smile was so mawkishly sweet, and he kept on blinking as if the sun were in his eyes. He bowed to each member of the family in turn, but it was as if he only bowed in order to draw himself up all the taller. When he came to Miss Sophie, his pale face flushed slightly and he whispered – or rather, lisped – a lengthy compliment in French. At table he hardly took his eyes off her, not even when speaking to someone else. Now and then she stole a glance at him; but I burnt my hand on the plates, so that today it is full of blisters – would it were only my hand that ached.

Thiele, Nov. 20th, 1711

Yes, it is true enough: there is to be a marriage. You only have to observe her ladyship. When she looks at Miss Sophie, she bends her head back like a duck that has filled its crop, rolls her eyes and closes them in turn, as if just about to fall asleep, and then quacks: '*Un cavalier accompli, ma fille! n'est ce pas vrai? et il vous aime, c'est trop clair?*'[39] Yes, alas, it is plain enough; and she returns his love, that too is plain. If only she may be happy.

Thiele, Dec. 4th, 1711

His Excellency has not yet derived much benefit from the chase. We have been out twice, but each time he has grown weary of it half-way through. There is a quarry at home in the manor that attracts him like a magnet. Alas! If only I had remained in Copenhagen!

Thiele, December 8th, 1711

Today the marriage was announced, and the wedding is to be in eight days time. Where shall I hide myself meanwhile? It is more than I can bear; whenever he puts his arm around her waist it is as if someone stabbed me in the heart . . .

Good Heavens! I believe Jens feels the same as I do. When I told him about the marriage he hammered his gun so hard on the ground that the butt broke in two, and then ran out onto the moors with the broken piece in his hand. So I am not the only fool in the world.

Thiele, December 16th, 1711

Miss Sophie is smitten with small-pox. Oh, how I tremble for her life! If only I could die in her place; but I cannot catch this illness more than once. Her lovely face is quite covered with blisters.

Thiele, December 19th, 1711

Here there is great sorrow and distress. Miss Marie is dead, and the master will not be comforted; but Her Ladyship speaks only of her funeral – how this is to be arranged. I suppose Miss Sophie will follow her sister, for she is very poorly. His Excellency, her betrothed, prepares to depart – *bon voyage!*

Thiele, March 13th, 1712

So I have risen at length from my bed of sickness. I thought it was going to be my last, and prayed to God with all my heart for deliverance. But I am to wander yet a while in this vale of sorrow – it is His will – let it be done! It feels as if I have arisen from the dead, and that those three months of sickness have lasted for three years. Yesterday I saw her for the first time since I was taken ill, and with reasonable composure; one should almost think that my sickness had cured me of my foolish infatuation.

She was a trifle pale and I don't think she looked very happy. Alas, she probably has no good reason to be so. His Excellency is surely a great libertine: the other day, through a crack in my door, I saw him grab hold of the mistress's maid, and that in a highly indecent manner. Oh, the poor young lady! If I were His Excellency I would worship her as an angel from Heaven.

Thiele, May 1st, 1712

His Excellency has gone away and let his betrothed remain here without him. He was probably tired of her already, and I believe – God forgive me! – also she of him. She does not seem to pine for him, for she is just as merry and *vive* as before – even more so; and yet now and again she seems a little haughty. Sometimes she treats me as if I were a beggar, and sometimes as if I were her equal. I almost believe she likes to poke fun at me – unfortunate wretch that I am! I have not come to my senses yet, for she can make me happy or sad just as she pleases.

Thiele, June 3rd, 1712

I shall never regain my health, the cheerfulness of my youth has left me. I feel languid and weary of soul and limb, and have no desire to do anything at all. I don't feel like hunting, and I don't feel like reading either; my gun and my Ovid are both equally dusty. French, which I once found so enjoyable, I have no wish to read or to hear – it is a false tongue!

Thiele, June 24th, 1712

I have exchanged bedchambers with Jens. He insisted on having mine, for he was afraid of looking out on the churchyard, the fool! He is sure to lie there for ever one day. I am quite pleased with the change; from my window here I can see the graves of my dear parents – they are in good hands – God bless their souls in Heaven! Over there is Pastor Søren's grave; there are already thistles growing on it – I shall have to clear them away!

Thiele, Dec. 13th, 1712

Her ladyship's maid has given birth to a little son. She has declared the father to be a lace-pedlar – but the whole house knows very well who the guilty one is. The young lady herself has jested about it. I don't know how she could; but she always makes light of things – that is not my nature.

Thiele, February 27th, 1713

Am I dreaming or am I awake? Have my senses deceived me, or was she really mine? Yes, she was mine. I have embraced her with these very arms, she has rested her head on my breast and covered my face with kisses – with passionate kisses. Now I should like to die, for I can never be so happy again. Oh, dear! What is the matter with me? What have I done? Oh, I don't know what I'm writing – I fear I may have gone out of my mind.

Thiele, March 5th, 1713

Let me recall those sweet moments. Let me truly consider how blissful I was; not until now do I begin to awaken as if from an intoxication . . .

The master returned from the hunt, and Jens had remained in the forest to dig out a hound that was stuck in a fox-hole. I knew very well that he would not come home before daylight, so I thought I would go and sleep in my old bedchamber. I had just dropped off when I was awakened with a kiss. Startled, I sat up and was about to cry out, when I felt a soft hand on my mouth, an arm around my neck and a sweet whispering voice . . . Good heavens! It was hers – I dare not even mention her name. Then . . . then . . . Oh, sinner that I am, inveterate sinner that I am – I have betrayed my master! And I cannot even repent it in my heart. Whenever I try to feel penitent, I am prevented by a secret rapture which makes mockery of my remorse. I can feel it: I long to repeat the misdeed I ought to curse . . . 'For ever mine!' were the first words I could utter; but then she tore herself out of my embrace with a stifled scream, and – I was alone. The door creaked and I sat up in bed; I began to wonder whether it hadn't been a ghost. Oh, why did she flee? Why, then, did she come unbidden, untempted? Has she loved me as I have loved her – silently, deeply and passionately?

Thiele, March 6th, 1713

O world! World! How false thou art! Honesty has totally vanished, virtue and honour are trampled under foot! Though why should I complain? Am I better than he is? Is my sin less because I believe my love to be the greater? Alas, I am only getting my deserts, the one is no better than the other – the one betrays the other. Ha! thou false woman, thou Potiphar's wife![40] It was therefore you cried out and fled when you heard my voice. So it was of old habit, a trodden path, when you sought out my bed – no, Jens's bed! Old love, old vice! Whereas I worshipped you – whereas I gazed upon you with awe, as upon a Holy Angel, you were whoring with my fellow servant!

It was midnight. Drunken with sweet memories I was strolling in the garden. I thought I saw something stirring on a shadowy path – I felt it must be her. I quickened my pace and hurried to the spot – it was her! It was indeed her – and how did I find her? On Jens's lap, with her arms around his neck. Hastily, they rushed from one another, and I stood there, feeling as if the ground would swallow me up. The sun found me in the same spot; I was freezing – trembling like an aspen leaf. Oh, thou wretched, thou false, thou depraved world.

Thiele, March 9th, 1713

I have seen her for the first time since that night of sin. A quick blush passed over her face. She kept glancing around the room, so as to avoid looking at me. I felt at once both hot and cold. The moment we were alone she walked hurriedly past me, saying, with half-closed eyes: '*Silence!*' She was out of the door before I even remarked the pressure of her hand.

Thiele, April 13th, 1713

The cat is out of the bag! The master, the mistress, the entire household, know it, and it was Mademoiselle Lapouce who found them out and betrayed them. The young lady loved to tease her, and she had born a silent grudge against her. No one had been aware that this crafty woman could understand a few words of Danish, and so she got wind of what was going on from some remark they had carelessly let fall in her presence. She followed the scent until she ran them to earth and caught them in the act. Heavens, what a commotion there was! His lordship ran around with his gun like a madman, threatening to shoot Jens, but Jens was already on his horse and far away. The young lady was locked up in the corner-room so that the master shouldn't lay hands on her. Oh Heavens! What will be the end of it? I tremble every time I hear his voice. My conscience condemns and makes a coward of me. I am so overcome with remorse and fear that love and jealousy have been driven from my heart. Alas! If only I were fifteen leagues under the ground!

Thiele, April 14th, 1713

Jens has been here. He entered my bedchamber in the night to hear how matters stood. He was like a drunken man, weeping and cursing in turn. 'If you tell anyone that I've been here', he said, as he left, 'you are a dead man!' He would most certainly keep his word; I shall indeed take care. But I wonder what he really wants? I suppose he doesn't even know himself.

Thiele, April 17th, 1713

The young lady is gone! She escaped out of a window last night. Jens must have been here to fetch her, for close on midnight someone encountered two persons on one horse, but it was too dark to determine whether they were both men. It was on the road to Viborg, and we had been out all day to a man, looking for them. We returned home without finding them. I heard that they had crossed Skiern Bridge, but I shall take care not to go too near them, you may be sure! Alas! What a world we live in! My poor master! This will surely be the death of him. He is in bed, and no one is allowed to go near him.

Thiele, April 20th, 1713

Today his lordship sent for me. Oh, Thou gracious Saviour! How pale and emaciated he was! He will not live, that I could plainly see. 'Morten!' he said, when I entered the room, 'is that you? Come over here!' As soon as I heard his voice I burst into tears. Formerly it had resounded as if from a barrel, and when he shouted out of the great door, 'Morten, bring the dogs!', it was as if the house would fall about our ears, and the chickens and ducks fluttered around in terror. But now he spoke so softly, so feebly, that my heart was fit to break. 'Morten!' he said, 'haven't you seen any snipe?' 'No, dear master,' I sobbed, 'I haven't been out at all.' 'Oh, haven't you?' he said, 'I shall not go out shooting again!' 'Why, yes!' I replied. 'God may yet help you.' 'No, Morten', he said, 'my days are soon told. Maybe – if only I still had Kresten!' At this, he pressed back two tears in his hollow eyes. 'Where is Vaillant?' he asked. 'He is lying in front of the fire,' I answered. 'Call him,' he said. The dog came and laid his head on the side of the bed. Looking sorrowfully at him, the master patted him at some length. 'You have been a true and faithful servant,' he said. 'You have never let me down. When I am dead you must shoot him and bury him under the big ash outside the churchyard. But take careful aim, and don't let him suspect what you have in mind – you must promise me that!' 'Yes, your lordship,' I replied. 'I don't want him given to strangers,' he said, as he sank back on the pillow. 'My hunter and Donner (his favourite gun) and my sword-belt – they are for you. You must never part with my Blis; when he grows so old that he can no longer eat, you must shoot him.' 'Yes, dear master,' I replied – I could scarcely speak for tears. 'And there on the table', he said, 'is a roll of money – that is for you, for you have served me faithfully and true. Go now, Morten, and pray to God for my sinful soul!' He gave me his hand and I kissed it, and then stumbled down to my own bedchamber. Oh, may God grant him a blessed end! He was a good and gracious master to me.

Thiele, May 3rd, 1713

So he too has gone to his last home! Now I no longer have a friend on earth. I shall not stay here; I must go out into the world to rid me of my melancholy thoughts. Poor Vaillant! When I took hold of my gun, he jumped around so friskily; he didn't know I was leading him to his death. No, never in my life had I fired such a shot. When I cocked the gun and he heard the click, he began to wag his tail and look around; he expected to see a quarry, and least of all suspected that he was in fact the quarry. When the shot had been fired and he was writhing in his last agony, I felt as if my heart would burst. Oh, my poor dear master! That was the last, the most onerous service I have done you.

Aboard ship off Thunø, May 17th, 1713

For the second time – perhaps the last – I am bidding you farewell, my beloved country. Farewell, you green woods, you brown moors! Farewell all the joys of my youth! It was with a lighter heart that I ploughed these wild waves two years ago. I had my good master then; but now he is in his grave, my young master likewise, and she – whom I should like to forget – is roving the wide world, God knows where or how. I too shall try my luck and eat my bread among strangers. Ay, I shall march to war – it will bring me either bread or death! Blis and I shall go together; he is my last friend on earth.

Sweden, June 13th, 1716

Here I am, a prisoner in a foreign land. This is what my sword has brought me to. My colonel and I thinned the ranks of the enemy, but we were only two against ten. Alas, my old Blis! You had to die – would that we had died together!

Stockholm, August 14th, 1717

This cannot go on much longer! They have dragged me around from one fortress to the other, trying to tempt or threaten me into entering their service. But I would rather starve to death in a dungeon than fight against my rightful King and master. More than anything I long for my freedom. I will seek and find it, or die in the attempt.

Norkjøping, February 3rd, 1718

So I became a Swedish soldier nevertheless! However much I was on my guard, concealing myself like a hunted animal in forests and on mountain crags, they found me at last. What was I to do? Better to be under God's open sky among swords and cannons than within the four walls of a prison! They have promised me that I should never have to fight against my countrymen, but only against the Muscovite – perhaps he has the right bullet with Morten Vinge's name on it.

Siberia, May 15th, 1721

The Lord my God! How curious are Thy ways! Many thousands of miles from Denmark I am wandering here in a harsh and dreary land; I walk over frozen rivers and wade in snow to my knees, while at home both woods and meadows are clad in their green summer dress. Outside the window of my old bedchamber the apple tree is now in bloom, the linnet chirps in the gooseberry hedge, the starling sits on the edge of the well whistling his merry tune and the lark is singing high up in the sky. Here wolves and bears are howling and grunting, while hawks and ravens are screaming and croaking in the black forests. Where, I wonder, does this wilderness end? Oh, when is this miserable life going to end?

Riga, September 2nd, 1743

Shall I ever live to see my native land again? For four and twenty long sorrowful years, four and twenty winters, I have hunted sable and marten in the Siberian forests! How weary of life I have been for so long – so long! But I shall wait patiently until my Lord and Saviour calls me to Him. Perhaps He will lay my weary limbs to rest in my native soil. Ah, there I see the

Danish flag, the precious sign of the Cross and of our salvation. Bless the Lord, O my soul: and all that is within me, bless His Holy name!

Falster, October 23rd, 1743

Again I have been close to death, and again I have escaped! In gale and storm I approached my beloved land. The waves smashed our ship and threatened to swallow us up; but the Lord delivered me, His hand upheld me – nor will He withdraw it from me now, though I wander, poor and half-naked, among strangers.

Corselidse, November 2nd, 1743

I have found a refuge, a shelter from the storms of the world: a noble and pious lord who has taken me into his service and promised to provide for me until the day of my death. So now I shall no longer change my abode before I am carried to my final resting-place.

Corselidse, May 1st, 1744

What lovely country this is! Everything in full bloom! Green woods and green meadows! Flowers everywhere! In Siberia it is still winter. Praise be to God for this change!

My master is greatly attached to me. I often have to sit for hours and tell him about the war and about all the countries through which I have wandered. And if he likes to listen, I'm willing to talk, for it pleases me to recollect the innumerable trials and tribulations I have endured.

Corselidse, July 2nd, 1744

Oh, Thou Father of mercy! Had I yet to drink of this bitter cup? Were the old wounds to be torn open anew? Ay, for such was Thy will. I have seen her. Her? Alas, no – not her! I have seen a fallen angel – a figure of darkness. I have often desired death, but now . . . now life is loathsome to me – I can write no more.

Corselidse, August 8th, 1744

It is not for my own pleasure that I take up my pen once more; but should anyone chance to light upon this diary after I am dead, he will come to see how sin rewards its children. On that distressing day I was enjoying a walk in our beautiful garden. As I pass the open gate, I see a man standing there whose face seems to me familiar, in spite of a bushy black beard streaked with grey and a sinister glance that almost terrified me. 'So you're here too?' he said with a strange smirk. My stick fell from my hand and I trembled in every limb – it was Jens! 'Good God!' I said. 'Am I to find you here? Where is Miss Sophie?' He answered with a loud oath: 'The Devil has taken the Miss and the Madam too, but if you want to see my dearly beloved wife, then she's down there weeding. 'Sofe!' he cried. 'Here's an old friend!' Then she half turned around – she was kneeling on the ground three paces away – and looked up at me for a moment, whereupon she resumed her weeding. I could not make out the slightest trace of emotion in her face – that face, that once so lovely face! How changed it was! Sallow, wrinkled and disgruntled, it looked as if she had never smiled in her life. A ragged bonnet with long tatters of black lace made it appear even darker. Dirty remnants of clothes that had once had been handsome and fine, hung about her heavy, ill-shaped body in rags. I felt as if I were about to vomit, and not a tear came into my eyes. I was seized with fear and loathing, as if suddenly confronted with a viper. I dared neither speak nor stir from the spot. Jens aroused me from my stupor. 'You see, she's not as beautiful now', he cried, 'as the time she crept into bed with you!' I shuddered. 'The gilding has worn off', he continued, 'but she still has her charming disposition. She's still haughty and spiteful, and how she can chatter! Hey, Your Ladyship! Come and talk to us!' She was silent and pretended not to hear, although he shouted loud enough. 'She doesn't choose to now', he said, 'but as soon as we get home, she'll start talking her head off. Could you spare enough for a measureful, Morten, for old time's sake?' I gave him something and walked in a daze back to the house. My master was standing by the garden door. 'Do you know these people?' he asked.

'Yes, God help me,' I replied. 'I used to know them many years ago.' 'They're a bad lot,' he said. 'She is ill-tempered and devilish, and he drinks like a fish. They have been living for a couple of years in a house down by the shore. He fishes, and she works some days in the garden here. People say she is of good family.' Not until then did my tears begin to flow and ease my heavy heart. I told him who she was, and his horror was as great as my distress.

Corselidse, September 14th, 1744

I doubt if I shall remain here. I no longer feel at ease, since I know I am near her, and often I cannot avoid seeing her. I have not spoken to her yet, for I shun her as an evil spirit. Jens seeks me out with an importunity that pleases neither me nor my master. When I smell his breath, which is always reeking with schnapps, it is like someone offering me poison to drink. He has told me their story – oh, how dreadful it is, how loathsome. They had wandered about in Denmark and Germany from one town to the next, he playing the horn and she singing and playing the lute. Thus they earned their living; and when that did not suffice she plied yet another trade, which it breaks my heart to think of. In time even that had to come to an end, and they would have died of want if my kind master had not taken pity on them. God forgive me, but I could wish myself back in Siberia.

Corselidse, May 1st, 1745

God bless my kind, generous master! He has become aware of my wish – to end my days in the place where I was born. And so – unknown to me – he has found me a good situation with the new people at Thiele. On Tuesday I shall set sail from Stubbekjøbing. God reward him for it, in all eternity!

At sea between Zealand and Samsøe, June 4th, 1745

'Fear not them which kill the body alone, but rather fear him which is able to destroy both soul and body.' I feel the power of these words of our Saviour. I felt more at ease when, in my youth, I faced the bullets of the Swedes on these same waves, than when I saw the fallen angel of my youth in the garden at Corselidse. Swords and bullets, stabs and blows, wounds and death are nothing in comparison to the perdition of the soul – to the destruction of an innocent soul. If at that time I had seen her beautiful body torn by wild beasts, it could not have wrung my heart as much as now, having found her ruined, depraved, an object of contempt, lost beyond redemption. As she knelt there digging in the ground, it seemed as if she buried my last hope, my last vestige of faith in honour and virtue. But I shall say, as the old Turk who shared my captivity in Siberia always used to say in the midst of the greatest suffering: 'God is great!' Yes, and merciful, too! He can and does accomplish far more than we poor human beings understand.

Thiele, July 4th, 1745

So at length I have entered my last winter haven! For more than thirty years I have been tossed on the wild ocean waves, only to end up where I began. What have I achieved? What have I gained? A grave – a resting-place together with my forefathers. That is something, and not so little at that. I have friends and acquaintances both above and beneath the ground. The apple tree still stands outside my window; it too has grown older – there's a canker in its trunk, the gales have bowed its head, and its branches are covered with moss like the grey hair on an old man's head. Beside the church wall I can see the big ash under whose roots I buried poor Vaillant. Thus I recognize many a tree, many a heather-clad hill and even the lifeless stones which have stood here unchanged for thousands of years, seeing one generation after another grow up and pass away. Now the generation I knew is also gone. New masters, new servants – I am a stranger, a foreigner among them all.

Thiele, Sept. 2nd, 1749

Today it is fifty-six years since I first saw the light of this world. Dear God, what has become of these years – these many thousands of days? Where are the delights of my youth? They are with the friends of my youth. It was at this time of the year that we used to enjoy the delights of the chase. What merriment there was when we set out in the morning – the huntsmen shouting and the hounds baying, and the horses stamping just as impatiently as we ourselves. Sometimes we went after the black grouse on the moors, sometimes after the wild game in the forest; with song and music we set forth, and with song and music we returned home. Now it is as quiet as a monastery here; the new master doesn't care for hunting. Silent and solitary, the gamekeeper goes out, and quietly he returns. This generation is cheerless as I am.

Thiele, January 12th, 1751

A calm, glorious winter night! Everything I see is blue or white. The moon has chased away the stars, wishing to shine alone. It shone just as beautifully many, many years ago when I was driving Miss Sophie. My tender soul shone just as brightly and merrily as the moon, and hers too was as pure and unblemished as this new-fallen snow. Now my soul is as dark as the moor when the snows of winter have melted, and hers – if she is still alive – must resemble a Siberian valley after a flood: darkly furrowed by streams of water, thickly strewn with tussocks, stones and fallen trees. 'Yea, Lord, Lord! When Thou with rebukes dost correct man for iniquity, Thou makest his beauty to consume away, like a moth: surely every man is vanity.'

Føulum, May 12th, 1753

On Sunday I took office for the first time as parish clerk of Thiele and Vinge. His lordship appointed me on his deathbed. Here I am living in my father's house, but I live here alone. All the friends of my youth have long since gone to rest; I alone remain, like a leafless tree on the moors; but before long I shall meet them again, and be the last of my family. These pages will be my only memorial. If, when I am dead and departed, any person should chance to read them, he will sigh and say: 'As for man, his days are as grass: as a flower of the field, so he flourisheth. For the wind passeth over it, and it is gone; and the place thereof shall know it no more. But the mercy of the Lord is from everlasting to everlasting.'

THE GAMEKEEPER AT AUNSBJERG

As a child I had to stay – or was rather incarcerated – on this estate more frequently and for longer periods than I wished. The owner, Counsellor Steen de Steensen, was in fact my mother's uncle. He and his wife – a Schinkel – had no children; I was named after him, and he was a kindly man. She . . . Yes, she was really fond of me . . . she was a 'thoroughbred', as they say. And we know that such people are prone to whims that not even the awareness of the 'permanent guillotine' is capable of eradicating – she wanted to dominate, no less.

'Where is your will, little Steen?' she would often ask me – though only when strangers were present. I was a doll, an automaton; and she had taught me to answer, 'In Grandmama's pocket.'

This poor boy's usual consolation was to tease, in her absence, her favourite dog Manille, which, between you and me, had an extremely peevish and irritable disposition. To my satisfaction, though, it once inadvertently came within range of the tether of an eagle – which was also imprisoned, though to a grassy spot in the garden; whereupon this king of birds murdered the favourite and ate him for lunch. By order of the reigning queen he was court-marshalled, of course, and the sentence – to be shot – was carried out there and then by the gamekeeper Vilhelm.

This same gamekeeper was *my* favourite; and I was never happier than when allowed to visit him in his room, examine his guns, play with his dogs, and listen to his hunting stories. His name was really Guillaume, which means the same in French as Wilhelm in German, and he was in fact a Frenchman. (I am well aware that I have a reputation for lying; and at this point too someone may perhaps accuse me of fabrication.

But that wouldn't worry me; I can authenticate this – and I'm a stickler for authenticity.) General Numsen, who had within living memory once commanded the Randers dragoons, had prior to entering Russian service been an officer in the French army, where the dragoon Guillaume had been assigned to him as orderly. And both Numsen and his orderly had grown so weary of the final 'dance' at Rossbach – which Mme. Pompadour's general didn't lead up the Rhine, because that *'der alte Fritz'*[1] did, but rather down it – and were so up to the neck in all the powder drifting from the French wigs, that they bid the petticoat-regiment farewell and left for Denmark.

Vilhelm was a stocky, square-built fellow with thick black hair, ditto eyebrows and small brown eyes in a broad, pale, though handsome face. Unlike most Frenchmen he had such a serious disposition that I can never recall having seen him

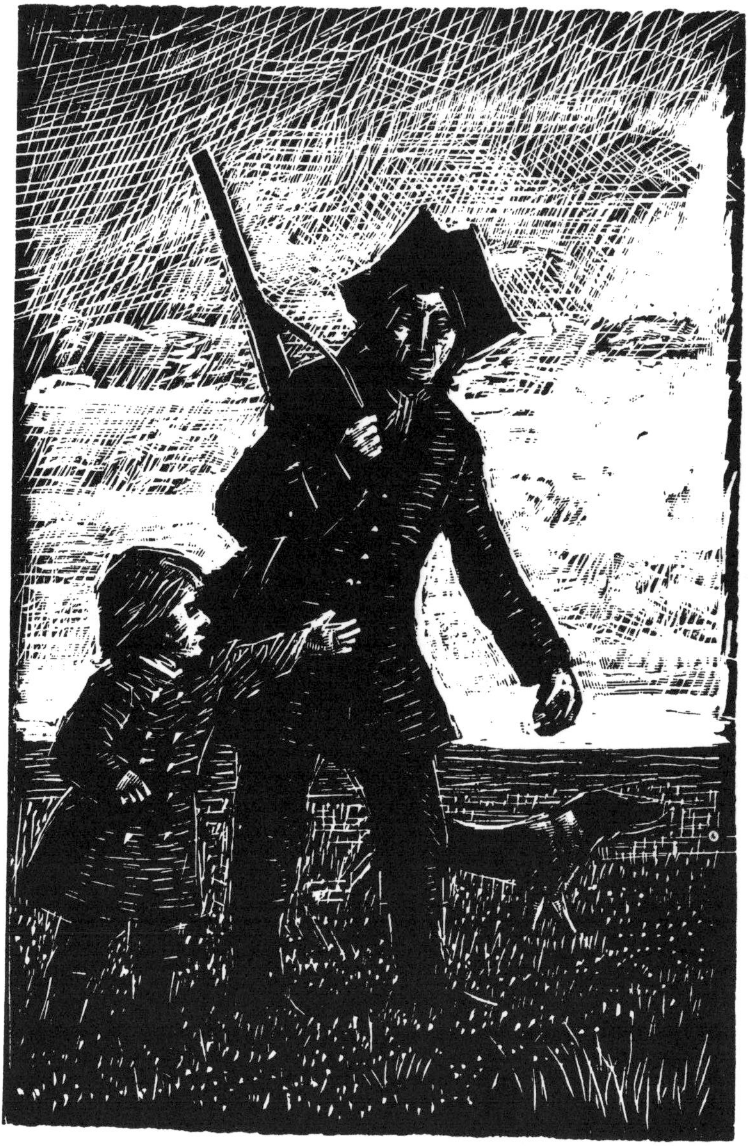

laugh. Even a smile was for him a rarity, and there was something about it that even put me off. Furthermore, he was taciturn and said no more than absolutely necessary, except on the occasions when he felt inclined to tell me something – and then his expression seemed quite different from normal.

    The master – as Grandpapa was usually called – paid more attention to Vilhelm than to the steward himself, always saying that he was 'as honest as the day'. Her ladyship didn't much care for him, and it seemed to me as if she deliberately avoided speaking to him; at any rate I often had to pass on her orders, even if he were no further away than from one door to the next. Vilhelm had almost as little to do with the other servants on the estate – though with one exception. This was a young and – according to those who knew – very pretty housemaid by the name of Mette. One might have thought she would have resembled him in temperament and demeanour. But, on the contrary, she was always good-natured and cheerful, and yet so proper in her behaviour that the valet – who couldn't do without, and never in fact lacked a bit of kiss-and-cuddle, first with one and then with the other – called her a prude when she and Vilhelm were out of earshot. The steward, the gardener and the bailiff called her names that were just as rude, though not of course in the presence of the master and mistress.

    I was often surprised, and couldn't understand why it was, that when Vilhelm and Mette were together he looked less grave and she looked more serious than usual; and even less why, after some while, both of them looked serious no matter whether they were together or apart. And this became even worse as time passed, until finally, when no one else but little me was present, I saw poor Mette crying. And when I asked her why she was crying she said she had toothache.... But more about that later. For the time being, by your leave, I shall relate something that occurred at the time when the maid began to suffer from toothache.

    The master had sent the gamekeeper down south – I don't recall where or why. On his way home in the late afternoon he comes riding to Them Inn, about four miles west of

Himmelbjerg. Leaving his horse to rest for a couple of hours, he sits down in the tap room between the bed and the big stove in order to take a nap in the warm. Shortly afterwards first one peasant and then another comes in and sits down at the table with a mug of ale and a pipe of tobacco; but not one of them notices the gamekeeper.

Now a few weeks previously there had been an accident in the neighbourhood: a pair of horses pulling a wood-cart had bolted and overturned the cart, crushing the head of the peasant girl who was driving it, and who was alone on the cart, against a tree. This event was the subject of the guests' conversation. Two of them had themselves been on the same forest outing, but had been so far behind that they had not seen how it actually took place. Not even a farm hand who was driving the cart after hers knew what had made the horses bolt, and none of those following after had been able to see anything of the two foremost carts when the accident occurred. The fact that the fellow hadn't seen anything either they could only explain by surmising that he must have been asleep.

As they are sitting talking about it, the very same man comes in and sits down at the table, and the others instantly start asking him to explain yet again how it had come about. After having wetted his vocal cords with a glass of schnapps and a draught of ale he complied with their request. But his report cannot have satisfied his listeners, because first one and then the other interrupted him, remarking that what he said now didn't tally in this or the other respect with the explanation he had given to start with. At last he grew angry, braced his back against the wall and shouted at the one then repeating the observation:

'What's the matter with you? You don't imagine I'm to blame for Karen's death, do you? That', he said, banging the table with his fist, 'you'll damned well have to prove!'

The man he addressed was quite taken aback and said no more. But one of the older men tried to calm the angry fellow down, assuring him that no one had implied or said that. At that very moment Vilhelm rushes out of his hiding-place, strikes a thundering blow on the table in front of the fellow, and roars, 'You did murder her – I shall prove it.' The horrified guests jumped up from their seats. But the accused slid down from the bench, and – with only his deathly pale face showing above the table – he stammered, trembling and with chattering teeth, 'I did do it – indeed, I wish to confess.'

The gamekeeper had not been asleep, of course, but had closely followed the whole conversation and become convinced thereby that this was the murderer. Appearing so suddenly, like a ghost or an avenging angel, to shake up his guilt-ridden conscience, the sinner's hard shell cracked – his enforced courage was crushed, his effrontery destroyed.

Tied and bound, he was taken before the district judge, to whom he explained that he had got the girl with child, that he had grown tired of her, and that her eternal reproaches and threats to disclose him and thus to prevent his intended marriage to another girl had made him decide that she must die. At a bend in the forest road, where both his cart and hers would for a few minutes be hidden by trees and bushes from those behind them, he jumped off and dealt her a lethal blow on the head with the back of his big axe, then lashed the horses with his whip; whereupon the latter, sensing that there was no one at the reins, made off at breakneck speed.

The criminal got the punishment he deserved; while Vilhelm acquired the general reputation of being 'someone who knew a thing or two' – in other words, a sorcerer.

It is not only in order to characterize the protagonist in this true story of mine* that I have described the murder and the scene of its discovery, but also because I am inclined to believe it to be connected with another death about which I shall presently relate. But first we shall return with the gamekeeper to Aunsbjerg.

A few days after his return the counsellor was sitting in the parlour hearing me repeat one of my lessons when his wife came storming in, leaving the door wide open. But when she reached the middle of the room she stopped, flung out both her arms and stood there as if nailed to the spot, with staring eyes and trembling lips.

'God preserve us!' he said, without getting up. 'Whatever is the matter, my dear?'

'Mette . . . Mette!' she gasped.

'What about her, dear?' he asked quite calmly.

'Mette is with child,' she stammered in dismay.

'Then, 'pon my soul (that was his only oath), she has been together with a man.'

---

* It is indeed true.

'She must leave . . . leave the manor!' she shouted. 'And that at once, he as well!'

'Who is this 'he', dear?' he asked.

'The gamekeeper,' she replied. 'The gamekeeper, dear heart . . . that wicked man!'

'My dear', he protested, ''Pon my soul, I do believe you're . . . I almost said . . . Vilhelm is as innocent as I am.'

'Yes, you say that, dear heart', she cried, 'because you think so highly of that wicked wretch. But he himself has admitted it. I have had my suspicions for a long time about that baggage – that there is something not quite right about her. So I take her to task in the pantry, question her closely and she confesses, though she won't on any account say who the guilty one is. But listen to this, dear heart! As I am pressing her with all my might, the pantry door opens, and who do you think is standing there in the doorway? Vilhelm, dear heart! And then he says . . . I didn't ask him, neither did the wench . . . And then he says, 'If Mette's expecting, then I'll be the child's father.' What do you say to that, dear heart?'

The counsellor rose in a state of agitation I had never hitherto experienced, saying, ''Pon my soul, I do believe we are in the dog days. . . . Tell them both to come here.'

She rushed out; he threw the book on the sofa and walked up and down the room, his hands clasped behind his back. Then in came the sinners – she with her face red from weeping, he with his customary quiet and grave demeanour. Her ladyship stood behind them with both fists planted in her sides, the counsellor in front of them with his hands still behind his back.

He scarcely looked at the girl, but fixed his eyes on Vilhelm's impassive face. 'Vilhelm', he said after a moment's pause, 'I would never have believed it of you . . . at your age . . . fifty to the day, I believe . . . and that young child . . .'

'My Lord', said the gamekeeper with imperturbable equanimity, 'may I not have a word with you in private, sir?'

After a moment or two's silence, the counsellor said, 'Follow me,' went into the adjoining room, Vilhelm after him – and the door was closed.

No one could hear what they were talking about in there, for they spoke very quietly and nothing was audible except an occasional 'Pon my soul!'

While these secret negotiations were going on – and I think they lasted half an hour – complete silence reigned in the parlour. Her ladyship threw herself on the sofa, glancing now at Mette and now at the closed door. Mette stood like a statue, staring fixedly down at the floor as the tears trickled down her cheeks, which were turning paler and paler. I sat on my own little stool, looking at my book and wondering what would be the end of it all – it was just as puzzling to me as hieroglyphics nowadays are to learned scholars.

When the counsellor re-emerged from the secret negotiations followed by his servant, he was wiping his nose – his eyes too, I believe – with his handkerchief. The latter's countenance seemed a bit brighter than before.

'My dear', the counsellor said, though slowly and hesitantly, 'these two are soon to be married.... You'll have him, won't you, Mette?' – the latter curtsied and bowed her head even deeper – 'And now we shall not speak any more of the past, my dear! ... Vilhelm, there's a house next to the smithy up in Vium ... it's unleased ... you can have it, so there's no reason why you shouldn't continue in my service.'

The gamekeeper bowed and said to his betrothed, 'Thank your master and mistress, Mette.' The latter rushed, sobbing, up to the master, curtsied first to him and then to her mistress, whereupon she tottered out of the room. The gamekeeper followed slowly after her. But when he reached the door, the counsellor called after him in a cheery fashion, 'Oh, Vilhelm, take a look at the alders and see if the snipe shouldn't have arrived tonight – it's the twenty-first today.' The gamekeeper nodded with a quiet smile, and went out.

Aunsbjerg lies in Lysgaard district and belongs to Sørslev parish. The church is of historical importance in that the Jutland nobility – so the story goes – gathered there when they conspired to renounce allegiance to King Christian II, Mogens Munk having been assigned by lot the perilous task of conveying this decision to His Majesty. But to me the churchyard is of even more vital interest – it also belongs to the dead. There you will find – and I hope it is still there – a fairly large mound surrounded by hewn stones, furnished towards the south with an iron grating that serves as a gate or wicket. Here lie the earthly remains of my younger brother and sister – who died in infancy – and of his lordship and his wife and several other members of the same family. When we attended the wedding of Guillaume Marteau and Mette Kjeldsdatter in Sørslev church the former two had not yet been born, while the latter were still very much alive.

The newly married couple moved to Vium the very same day. I recall, however, that after having escorted his wife to their new home, Vilhelm returned to the manor the same evening, though perhaps rather late, and that it hadn't upset my gracious grandmother. And this I understood just as little as her anger when, shortly afterwards, he named his son after me.

Everything returned to normal again, except that sometimes, when the weather was fine, I was allowed to take part in the hunts – hunts in which the game is driven by dogs or beaters towards the huntsman, who is stationary. I was told to stand behind my grandfather, each time with the admonishment that I was not to move. And I was more disposed to obey this order than when 'dear Grandmama' glued me to the stool at home.

Just as Vilhelm, after his marriage, seemed to have got even further into his master's good books, I got even further into Vilhelm's on account of my so early awakened aptitude for hunting. But I must get on with my story, all the more so because I am anxious to get what follows over and done with.

One autumn day the gamekeeper was told to ride out onto the moors to shoot grouse. He didn't come back in the evening – he had presumably stayed in Vium. But he didn't return the following day either. So in the evening a messenger was sent up to his wife – she hadn't seen him since the morning of the previous day when he had dropped by on his way. Then Grandpapa began to worry, having good reason to fear an accident; and that same evening two reliable men were sent out on the moors to search for him and to make enquiries in the settlement villages[2]. Late the following morning they returned with the report that two days previously he had called on the innkeeper at Haverdal and obtained some fodder for his horse and something to eat for himself and his dog, and that from there he had set off early for Aunsbjerg. At that the counsellor mounted his horse, and rode off accompanied by his steward and a couple of foresters. He seemed grave and anxious, and I already began to weep for Vilhelm.

For me it was a long day. Towards evening they returned, followed by two carts. On the first lay the dead body of Vilhelm, on the second his dead horse; his dog trailed behind them with drooping head and empty stomach.

Out on the moors, where nowadays the royal forest stands, there was at that time nothing but heather. But the work of preparing the ground started the same year in which the events I have just related took place. Even today the strip of land that lies a couple of thousand feet west of the forest ranger's house, and which was the first to be reclaimed for forestry, is known as 'the old plantation'. According to the rules of forestry, all over this area square pits had been dug, the surface layers of peat piled up beside them. It was here that poor Vilhelm was at last found after a long search on the vast moors, which were quite hilly in those parts. His pointer was their guide.

After having first tried in vain to find trace of him in the settlement or from the few scattered heath-dwellers of Vium parish, and then in the heather-covered valleys and peat-pits, they had suddenly heard the pitiful baying of a hound far away in the distance. They rode in the direction of the sound, which was repeated at short intervals; and as they drew near, the counsellor cried, "Pon my soul, it's Vagtel!' A bit closer, they caught sight of the white dog, which now poked its head upwards and howled and now lay down and disappeared in the heather again. They hurried to the spot. There, among the pits in the newly started plantation lay both hunter and horse, the former slightly in front of the horse's head and the dog by his side. Presumably the horse must have been ridden carelessly among these pits and have stumbled, and the rider had been flung over its head and broken his neck. Both bodies had already begun to putrefy. But the counsellor took a different view of the matter. By order of the court he had some investigations carried out; but nothing came out of them nonetheless. There was indeed a hole in the horse's chest, but it could have fallen against a sharp stone; and in any case the stench became worse and worse, and no one would or could undertake a post-mortem examination of either.

The decision to bury the gamekeeper's body could now no longer be postponed. I was present among the gatherers when my late father flung the first three spadefuls of earth on the coffin and pronounced the words that consign to corruption and transfiguration. But the grave was neither filled in nor patted down until several days afterwards, when the counsellor realized that all his efforts to find out anything further were fruitless.

The horse was buried on the same day in the paddock where it had been laid, while the dog ... Dear reader, whosoever you may be, do not take offence at the womanish weakness of a poor old poet. And do not laugh either, even though you may well believe him to be entering his second childhood.... The dog Vagtel, my dearest playmate in that stern Aunsbjerg – he who had so many a time shared my bread with me and who had more than once found and brought me a lost handkerchief or glove.... Aye, I admit it readily, I wept over Vagtel.... Was it for Vilhelm's sake? Very likely, I hardly know myself. But as long as Vilhelm's body lay unburied the dog kept vigil beside him. He would have followed him to the grave, but was much too weak for that. We closed the gate on him; whereupon he dragged himself out into the paddock and lay down on the spot where the horse was buried. We tempted him with the tastiest of morsels ... he turned his head away ... he starved and grieved himself to death ... he was buried beside the horse ... Grandpapa wept over him too.

But there was someone who wept even more than I did – Vagtel was not the only one to grieve himself to death for Vilhelm. Not only while the grave was still uncovered, but also long after it had acquired its green coverlet the widow visited it every evening to mourn – she could no longer weep, for she had no tears left. The grave lay a little to the north of the church tower . . . I would be able to find the place today just as surely as half a century ago. . . . There she would sit leaning against the wall, her hands folded in her lap, staring with mute despair at the mound that concealed the friend who had been so cruelly snatched from her. My father, the pastor of Vium, used to visit her every day, but she turned a deaf ear to his attempts to console her. 'My only friend on earth!' . . . Those were her only words.

The child suffered from its mother's anguish. It pined away . . . three weeks after the father's death it was laid beside him. This second loss made no impression on the widow; she had no feeling for the tiny body and cast it only a casual, apathetic glance. The women in the neighbourhood had to see that it was clothed and prepared for burial.

Scarcely a month elapsed before the mother lay on the other side of her husband.

Nine years had passed. I was in the top class at school, and was visiting my great-uncle at Liselund during the summer holidays. Liselund was a small farm on the Aunsbjerg estate where he spent his last days after having sold the manor house and all that went with it.

I had to account for my scholarly progress, and for much else that the inquisitive old gentleman liked to hear. During the course of the conversation we came inadvertently to speak of former times, and one recollection from my childhood years led to the other. So it was not at all strange that we came to think of the chain of events with which the reader is now familiar. It was I who brought it up, expressing my desire for any possible information about what still seemed to me obscure – aye, even somewhat sinister.

The old man regarded me, blinking his red-rimmed eyes. 'H'm!' he said. 'I'm not so sure that you would benefit from knowing these things – and yet – it may well be so. In God's name, I shall reveal to you what I know. Consider it well, and learn a good lesson from this luckless story.'

He was silent a while longer, bent his head, took out his

snuffbox and tapped the side of the box three times – as is right and proper when taking a pinch with delicacy. But he didn't do so; he rested the box on his knee, raised his head, and, staring at his favourite gun, which hung on the opposite wall, he said:

'That gun there . . . I hardly use it any more . . . my eyesight is no longer up to it . . . it used to belong to Guillaume de

Martonniere ... *de Martonniere!* Take note of that, my son! I acquired it in exchange for another gun, which was in fact better but didn't lie so well in my hands. And in exchange I also gave him that powder horn you see there, inlaid with silver ... I bought it back when his effects were auctioned. ... It is now nineteen years since he came to me from my brother-in-law at Hald Manor. I have never had a better gamekeeper, nor a better man in my service.' At this he brushed away a tear, saying, 'My eyes are running badly these days. ... We're going to have bad weather. ... Fetch me the eye drops, my boy – they're on the stove in there.' I did so; he bathed his eyes, and continued, 'You remember, of course, when he took that murderer and miscreant by surprise in Them Inn and, with his ferocious manner, forced him to confess?' – I nodded – 'But you probably don't know that the rascal was keeping company with Mette – the girl Guillaume married – and that he was the father of the child she bore?'

'No!' I exclaimed, in horror.

'H'm!' he went on. 'Surely you were at the manor that day when my late lamented wife discovered that the girl was pregnant, and when Vilhelm was together with me in the little room beside the parlour door?'

'Yes, indeed.'

'It was then that he explained himself, and gave me a good and clear account of what I am now going to tell you. ... When the murderer was being questioned Vilhelm had to attend several times in order to give evidence. Finally, just before the verdict was to be pronounced, the district judge admonished the criminal to confess anything else he might have on his conscience. And for the first time he burst into tears and was for a while so overcome with emotion that he couldn't speak. The judge told his clerk to dip his pen; but the sinner said, "What I have to confess is something for which only the all-merciful God can punish me, so there is no point in writing anything about it. I also wish to ask if I might be alone with the district judge and this man," – he meant Vilhelm – "for otherwise I wouldn't be able to say a word.' The judge complied with his request. And then he revealed that his true love, and the one he would have married if the Devil hadn't set a trap for him, was Mette Kjeldsdatter – at that time our housemaid. He had in fact been in service here, in the days when Hansen held the lease, and had become friendly with her. It was Whit Sunday, then, and they were merrymaking in the grove, as they did every year, and it was on this occasion that she allowed him to take advantage of her.... Alas, my dear son ... mark my words ... sin is the ruin of mankind.... Of course they would have got married, because he was truly fond of her and both their parents were comfortably off. But it so happened that shortly afterwards he attended a wedding in his home district, and there he also did amiss with the other girl, whom he subsequently murdered in order to marry Mette. "I beg and beseech you" – those were his final words to Vilhelm – "It is you who are sending me to the scaffold ... that I'm not complaining about ... I thank you for it ... but I beseech you for Jesu' sake to do whatever lies in your power to console Mette and to alleviate her great distress and misery, and you must never reveal that she has been got with child by such a great wrongdoer to any living soul – all excepting the master of Aunsbjerg, that is, if you think it might be to her advantage."

'I was of course greatly shocked on learning this' – the old man continued – 'and asked him what he had a mind to do. He passed his hand over his forehead and said, "I have deprived the girl of her sweetheart – although that I can never regret – but she is innocent of his crime, and it is my duty to compensate her as far as I can. Besides ..." – at this his countenance took on a gloomier expression than I have ever seen before or since – "besides ..." – at this he shuddered, walked swiftly over to the window as if to take a breath of fresh air, then turned briskly about, and asked, "Are you satisfied with my decision, sir?" And I not only answered this question in the affirmative but assured him that I respected him all the more for it. So that is how that short-lived and joyless marriage came about.

'Never as long as I live will I forget the morning when he was killed. Before he rode away he said he wanted to speak to me. And then he says calmly and philosophically – as if he were speaking of the weather – "Counsellor Steensen, sir", he says – he wasn't accustomed to addressing me by name – "if anything should happen to me today or any other day, and I should not be able to speak to you again, for the sake of the kindness you have always shown me, I wish to ask if you will comply with the request I have addressed to you, and which you will find in my pocket book. It lies in the middle drawer on the right-hand side of my bureau, and here is the key." These words made me feel ill at ease, for surely you don't doubt that there are such things as forebodings, my son; and these, as you know, proved not to be wrong. Well, I took the key, and explained to him whereabouts I wanted him to shoot the grouse that time, and he rode off.'

Again the old man had to resort to the eye drops, but this time it took somewhat longer before they helped. Finally, he went on to say, 'I had an instant suspicion that he had met with a violent death, and likewise a suspicion as to the name of the perpetrator, who could be none other than the brother of the other murderer – not so much because Vilhelm had pointed the latter out, but because he had caught the lad poaching and taken away his gun. For I have forgotten to tell you that this rascal had acquired a house out there, in a most convenient situation for that trade. And he came from a district – in the neighbourhood of Silkeborg, Them and Matrup – where poaching was rife, and still is, I believe. Presumably, when Vilhelm had set off from Haverdal, on a path skirting the old plantation, he had caught sight of the poacher in there – it was a good place to lay in wait for the red deer when they went to water in Aaresvad brook – and had made after him. And when the villain realized that he couldn't escape he had fired his gun, and hit the horse. But even if a bullet had been found inside that half-rotten cadaver, whose bullet would it have been?'

I wept again – after so many years – for my poor dear Vilhelm; and when the old man saw this he had to resort to the eye drops again. 'But not until his body had been laid out on its straw-covered bier,' he continued, 'did I come to think of the key he had given me and open his bureau. Here, take my key and go into my study and open my writing-desk; in the bottommost drawer in the middle there is a piece of folded paper tied up with black silk ribbon – bring it here!'

I did so.

'Fetch me my spectacles . . . but, no – you can read it yourself, but aloud, please.'

I read: 'Should it be the will of providence that I die an unexpected and sudden death, before, that is, I have been able to take any decision as regards my possessions, then I hereby request Counsellor St. de Steensen to dispose of them as follows: I bid him keep my few books in memory of me; my clothes, hunting implements, or whatever else can bring in money shall be sold, and the proceeds thereof shall belong to my wife, or in the event of her death, to the child, or if it too should die, to her next of kin; finally, in a secret compartment, there is a small package of letters that the counsellor shall in the first place retain, and as to what further should be done with them, instructions will be found in the package itself. The secret compartment may be found simply by applying pressure with the point of an awl . . .' – the rest was illegible due to some ink having been spilt on it.

'The cat did it . . .', said the old man. 'It jumped up on the table as I sat there reading, and knocked over the inkwell. But you will see below that he has signed himself "Guillaume de Martonniere". So he was in fact a nobleman. But I haven't been able to find the drawer, however hard I searched for it.'

'But you still have the bureau?' I asked.

'I most certainly do, for I bought it at the auction I arranged after his death. I haven't been able to make up my mind whether to chop it to pieces, not least because there is no sign at all of any secret drawer, for all the compartments seem to be of equal size and to extend right to the backing. If he really has possessed the documents he refers to, he must have kept them somewhere else.'

Thus ended his account, and mine must do likewise. When he died, and his effects were sold, I was far away, and I don't know what happened to the bureau, or whether it still exists. But should this be the case, and one of my readers should chance to know of its whereabouts, then it would be doing me – and possibly others too – a favour if he or she would inform me. For I am convinced that the letters concerned must be found in this piece of furniture, and are likely to contain information about Guillaume de Martonniere's early life and experiences, and to reveal to us how this French nobleman came to end his days as a simple gamekeeper in the service of a Jutland nobleman.

Dear readers, do not be vexed because this little story, which can scarcely be regarded as more than a lengthy anecdote, is so fragmentary, mysterious and sorrowful. Is not all earthly knowledge fragmentary? Is not all our wisdom mysterious, and the greater part of our experience . . . aye, let it be stated here ... sorrowful indeed? Many a time in my boyhood I would stand in Vium churchyard in the place where Mette had sat looking at the graves of her husband and child. I sat there when the sun had set behind Lyshøj hill in the northwest and listened to the dirge of the bittern down by Bastrup lake. I too was sad, but my grief contained no bitterness, and still less any doubt or fear. There was something ... nay, there was much ... that resembled joy – that was indeed joy. An animal does not mourn, except perhaps in human company – *grief is the prerogative of man.*

ALAS, HOW CHANGED!

Since I am a useless nitwit, only tolerated because I don't do any harm – that is to say, direct harm, for sensible people would say that my poetic drivel does indirect harm in more ways than one – and on account of my levity have never been able to acquire a permanent position (once I did nevertheless set my heart on becoming a fire-warden, another time I aspired to the office of bell-ringer, and a third time I contemplated becoming a gravedigger and undertaker, though each time in vain); and since I have nothing particular to do, I have plenty of time to see a bit of the world, and I make as good use of this as I can.

THE VISIT

No sooner had I returned from my visit to Copenhagen in the spring, where I resumed my acquaintance with a friend of my youth, the fortunate Counsellor S, than I decided to visit another old friend, who lived in a quiet, tucked-away spot in the north of Jutland. I had witnessed domestic bliss in the capital; now I hastened to seek it in a rural backwater. I had not seen my reverend friend, now Pastor Ruricolus, for more than twenty years, but he, Counsellor S and I had previously made a fine trio. We were sworn brothers, all three of us – jolly fellows, who enjoyed our youth in every respectable and acceptable way; but Ruricolus was the most elegant of us, both in dress and in manner. I wouldn't exactly have called him a dandy (and even less a fop), but he was always dressed in the latest fashion, and – as my late lamented mother used to say – he always looked so sleek. He had mastered the art of tying his cravat and the knee-bands of his black silk breeches to a perfection, and all his garments bore the hallmark of perfect symmetry. When we went walking on a summer Sunday in Frederiksberg Gardens it was he who attracted the most glances from the ladies, even though S was also a handsome fellow, and I was five-and-a-half inches taller than either of them.

But to be honest, I must confess that it was not only the longing for a friend of my youth that drove me there: nineteen years ago, in that district where he was now living, I had experienced my twentieth love affair. It was there that I met Maren the Second* – the lovely, angelic Maren Lammestrup, the pearl of all the Vendsyssel girls. It was there, for the twentieth time, I lost my tender heart – and, for the twentieth time, retrieved it safe and sound. Permit me, fair reader, to relate my innocent adventure:

Ruricolus and I made a summer excursion from within the city ramparts in order to spread a few gleams of light over the Vendsyssel peninsula. (Our voyage to the town of Aalborg deserves a separate description, which, with the aid of the Muses, I shall not fail to produce as soon as I have studied our great masters of that art and perfected myself in the style of travelogues.) We two Copenhageners – I a native, he a naturalized one – created a stir on the Great Marsh; our broad-brimmed hats, short waistcoats and long trousers attracted well-deserved admiration. Only Squire Lammestrup of Tyreholm Manor – a rough, uneducated and vulgar person – made so bold as to scoff at our dress. It was the first time anyone in Vendsyssel had seen long yellow nankeen trousers, with matching gaiters whose points reached right to the toes. That boor compared us to feather-footed pigeons; his daughter Maren, that sweet dove, found a more flattering simile – in our loving tenderness and amorous cooing. To these same yellow gaiters I even attributed – and probably not without good reason – a good portion of the success we two cavaliers had with her and the other Vendsyssel girls.

My heart is like tinder . . . no, that metaphor halts, for though

---

* Not to be confused with Maren the First, daughter of the town musician.

it catches fire easily it doesn't burn; tinder burns only once, and my heart any number of times. . . . My heart is like gunpowder . . . no, that isn't right either, for it catches fire at once, though burns gently and quietly, without smoke and without explosions. . . . So, my heart must be like asbestos . . . h'm, that won't do either, for asbestos doesn't burn at all. . . . Well, then, without a metaphor or any other figure of speech I shall say that I fell head over heels in love with that charming maid and sweet rosebud, Maren Lammestrup – at very first sight.

There was to be a haymaking feast at Tyreholm on the very same day we arrived at Kringelborg parsonage, where my Ruricolus's father lived. His Reverence received us most cordially:

'Welcome, Hans Mikkel!' he shouted at his son. 'Who's that fellow you've brought with you?'

Hans Mikkel told him. The good pastor shook my hand, and said, 'Welcome, Mr Copenhagener! What can I offer you? A schnapps? . . . Hey there, Barbara, bring some schnapps and a bite to eat! . . . You've come just at the right time, lads, for there's to be some merrymaking at Tyreholm this evening. . . . Well, Mr Copenhagener, what use can we put you to? Can you play Loo?'

'Indeed.'

'That's excellent! Can you shoot a hare?'

'No, I'm afraid not.'

'Shame on you! That's bad. . . . Can you smoke tobacco?'

'No, not that either, pastor.'

'Well I'll be damned! That's really too bad . . . but you can learn. Can you drink a tart?'

'I can eat a tart.'

'Aha! You don't even understand that *Terminus technicus*. . . . Can you stand a punch?'

'H'm – if it isn't too hard. I'd have to put it to the test.' (I still didn't realize what he meant.)

The good man laughed until the perspiration stood in beads on his round, ruddy-brown face.

'You just wait,' he said, still laughing. 'When you get to Tyreholm Miss Maren will introduce you to the Jutland tea-punch; she knows how to brew it!'

At that moment a large hound came bounding in. The pastor turned quickly from me to the dog, planted both fists in his sides and shouted, 'Well I'll be jiggered! Where have you come from? Are you alone, Spy, or is your master with you? You've been down in the goose-marsh, eh?'

While he was still examining the dog, its owner – a local squire – appeared, and offered to accompany the pastor to the feast. Both the good gentlemen immediately became engrossed in a profound discussion about hunting, and I remember that they both dwelt at length on the maxim, that the cunning of the wild duck almost matches that of the fox, which statement they illustrated with many a shining example. Meanwhile the carriage drew up, and all five of us – Spy included – set off for Tyreholm.

A VILLAGE BEAUTY

One could scarcely say that the formalities were observed at the old manor house mentioned above. There was nothing left of the old aristocratic pomp and circumstance but the bare walls, and the present owner hadn't even the air and dignity of a lackey. Not that he lacked haughtiness and vanity – far from it! But it was not the noble pride that is founded on parchments, family trees, stars and garters. Squire Lammestrup was proud of his money, and that alone. He had a yardstick of silver according to which he classified everyone without regard to standing: a pauper was a pauper irrespective of his class, and in those parts a good man was synonymous with a rich man, a poor man tantamount to a gypsy. I still have a vivid picture of his corpulent body as he stood at the door, his hands in his coat-tail pockets. His fat shiny face grinned at us with complacence and cunning, but he didn't stir from the spot until we had all alighted from the carriage. Then he slowly extended his broad fist, first giving Counsellor Svirum (Spy's hunting companion) his whole hand, and then Pastor Ruricolus two fingers – the two of us getting a nod between us.

'Have you seen my bullocks?' were the first words I heard from his lips; and since the answer was in the negative he continued with an even happier smile, 'Then you shall damn well see some good stock – they're no yearlings! Come, they're right outside the house.' As he spoke he put his hands in his pockets again and waddled off; the counsellor and the pastor followed him in respectful anticipation, while young Ruricolus and I remained standing there in bewilderment. When he reached the middle of the courtyard, Squire Lammestrup half turned to us and shouted: 'I presume you young fellows have no knowledge of such things. You can go and sit with the women in the meantime.'

We did so. And as fate would have it, one of these was to absorb my attention so completely that I forgot all others but her; and this one was indeed a *non plus ultra* of rural beauty – I saw at first glance that she was the most perfect example of her kind. I don't think I had ever seen such an abundance of beauty – blushing and buxom, yet contained in the loveliest of curves. But don't whatever you do imagine a plump, chubby-faced milkmaid! She was no 'Miss Flamborough', no 'Betty Bouncer' who could be divided without stinting into two young ladies! No, Miss Lammestrup was truly a pattern of graceful proportions as far as face and figure were concerned. And as for her soul – believe me, dear reader, I am by no means ironical when I say that this Jutland Maren was indeed exceptionally well-educated, which I soon discovered after a few brief conversations. She had read and digested her Lafontaine, and I needed only to mention 'Lotte' or 'Marianne'[1] to bring tears into her sky-blue eyes. Added to which she danced like a fairy, sang like an angel and played her piano – probably the only instrument of its kind to be found in the whole of Vendsyssel – with taste and accomplishment. In what hothouse this lovely wild flower had been cultivated I could not say; but one thing is certain – Squire and Mrs Lammestrup had had no hand in it.

I have already said – and no one is likely to find this surprising – that I instantly lost my heart to this wonderful girl. I must add that I am not accustomed to giving away my apple without having a pear in sight, and so on this occasion too I counted on a fair exchange; for quite apart from the friendliess that shone from her beautiful eyes when they first lighted on my person, she soon showed several unmistakable signs of a budding passion, of which I shall only mention the three most conspicuous:

Firstly, I noticed that when I struck my favourite pose . . . (with bent knees, the left one well in front of the right, the right hand on my hip, the left fist in my side with elbow bent forwards, shoulders likewise thrown forwards and slightly raised, head drooping, with wide-open eyes and mouth drawn up towards the nose to produce a disdainful expression – what the French call *dédaigneux* – somewhat like a soldier charging with his bayonette) . . . that when I stood like that, she whispered secretively to one of the other young girls, glancing over at me and smiling.

Secondly, when we went out in the hayfield, where we were to make a haystack in return for our share in the feast, and took the opportunity of pelting each other with hay, I was nearly always spared, though at the expense of my friend Hans Mikkel. My sweet Maren threw the first handful at his head, and all the other girls followed suit. He defended himself, and I came to his aid like a brother, but in vain! – the wild women charged at him alone, and, stumbling, he was instantly buried under a mountain of hay, while we on our part had lost the battle. I felt really sorry for the loser when I saw him standing there, brushing and picking all the straw and moss off his fine clothes, surrounded by seven laughing amazons, none laughing louder than my roguish Maren.

I observed the third and most obvious sign of the girl's love later during the dancing. It was then that the 'jump-step', as it was called, was in fashion, and I had really become quite proficient at it. The strange charm of this dance consisted in long leaps and vigorous kicks with head bent sideways over one shoulder, whereby the dancer butts his way forwards as if through a tightly-packed crowd. In this I had no equal – I could leap as much as four to six feet, and my fellow dancers took great care not to get too close to me. But that is understandable: such movements are pretty violent, and made me sweat a great deal. The dear girl did not fail to observe how hot I was after having danced the first dance with her. When I then asked her for the next dance – which was to be a waltz – she excused herself, though in the most courteous and amiable manner. And why? – solely out of delicate consideration for me; because towards Hans Mikkel she was not nearly so compassionate – she immediately promised him the next dance. I noticed with secret delight how the little minx kept on dancing with him to the very last, solely in order to wear him out, and to defeat him – if possible – in two different ways in one day (see the hay battle). But there is surely no need to cite further proof; my readers must already have discerned the state of Maren Lammestrup's innocent little heart. I rightly considered it my property, but I deliberately postponed the sweet hour of mutual declaration; it's so nice to have something to look forward to.

THE HAYMAKING FEAST

I have already said that I make tremendous jumps when dancing. No one can object to that; but to jump in my story may not please the thoughtful reader. For that reason I shall now – with due apologies for the long jump-step my heart has made with my pen – return to the country feast at Tyreholm and describe it soberly in the correct order.

The tea-punch, therefore, will be the first object of our attention. (Since the recipe for this extremely popular drink is no longer a secret, I shall not dwell on its description.) Here, then, in front of the steaming urn, Maren Lammestrup, the queen of the feast, sat brewing and handing out cups to our host, the counsellor, the pastor and five or six other gentlemen, until they in turn became steaming engines, and had equally many tobacco-engines running. I couldn't refuse to sit with them, but as soon as I had consumed my 'tart' I hurried out into the fresh air, for I was beginning to feel sick. The punch, the smoke of the vilest Virginia tobacco coupled with the conversation – which was quite bestial, for it was solely about bullocks, horses, hounds, duck and other wild animals – all had such an overwhelming effect on me that I had to seek solitude and to cool my forehead against the old and venerable walls of Tyreholm.

Since I well knew that just as honourable as it is to be able to drink a lot, it is equally despicable not to be able to stomach it, I endeavoured to put on a nonchalent air when I returned to the steam-engines. But I had only moderate success, for my host, who must have found my sudden exit somewhat suspicious, fixed his big milky-blue eyes on me, took his pipe out of his mouth – however loth it was to be removed – and said with a broad smile: 'I think my good friend looks a wee bit pale; I fear that Maren has put too many hops in the pot.'

This sally evoked general laughter, first on the part of the originator, and then from the entire tea-punch party. I kept a straight face and joined in the laughter, assuring them after the final burst that my indisposition was more the result of the journey than of the potency of the punch. The arrival of several guests cut short this scene, so amusing for all the others.

After the new arrivals had also received their share of the Vendsyssel nectar, the entire company made for the meadow. And it was here that the battle I have already described took place. I shall therefore skip this over and go straight to the dance.

The music for the latter was primitive – a single fiddle. Our solo fiddler, I recall, distinguished himself more by his vigorous bowing than by grace of execution, and made up for the lack of other instruments with a kind of double-stopping the like of which I had never experienced at the hands of any other maestro. In addition to this he had certain curious mannerisms, the novelty of which deprived Maren – Terpsichore – of half my attention. He kept the beat with both head and foot, accompanying his instrument with a kind of nasal tone that greatly resembled the muted snuffling of a doleful trumpet. Nevertheless everyone danced right merrily to this music until the early hours, when some of the company suggested playing parlour games for a change, these as usual accompanied by much kissing. We 'confessed', 'went a-begging', 'stood at the foot of the altar', 'ground mustard seeds', 'hung' and 'fell in the well' until the carriages drew up at the door; and with a heart as soft as melted wax I took my leave of Tyreholm and its enchanting fairy, the lovely Maren Lammestrup.

Should anyone wish to know how her father, the counsellor,

the pastor and the other gentlemen passed the night, I can only say that from the two card tables in the corners of the ballroom I constantly heard mysterious expressions – which for the uninitiated, would seem puzzling – such as 'clubs', 'diamonds', 'spades', 'hearts', 'pass' and 'loo'; 'I'll keep them', 'take the trick', 'Pam', 'I've got him', and so on. And every now and again a blow on the table, an oath, a roar of laughter or even a moment of deep silence would announce some important occurrence or other. Two or three times Pastor Ruricolus shouted loudly, 'Well, I'll be jiggered!' from which I concluded that His Reverence must have paid a large and undeserved penalty.

On their departure the counsellor invited all the gentlemen present to a duck-shoot on the lake at Svirum Manor.

I cannot conclude this chapter with equanimity before I have acquainted the reader with a reflection that has nearly always presented itself on such occasions. To be sure, it is neither pleasant nor cheerful, but it is natural and corresponds to one's mood after a wakeful, if not exactly dissipated night.

What a change – I thought – the space of a few hours can bring about! We are never more aware of how quickly we are affected by the swiftness of time – which usually seems to us slow, gradual, measured and almost imperceptible – than precisely on the morning after a ball. Where now is that merriment, that childish delight, that sweet anticipation with which the dancers met – that decorum with which they greeted one another and took their places for the first dance? How trim and neat both the ladies and the gentlemen were! Not a ribbon, not a flower, not a pin out of place; not a speck of dust on the white dresses or black coats; not a crease, not a wrinkle that wasn't intentional; every frill, every ribbon fell as it ought to; not a cravat that wasn't snowy white and fastened neatly under the chin, or a 'cockscomb' that lacked its appropriate height; not a ringlet that didn't curl, glossy and shining, in its appointed place – a snare for any unwary male heart. With sparkling eyes and softly blushing cheeks, the row of lovely girls stood waiting impatiently for the first signal. Attentive, almost solemn, the gentlemen observed the steps of the leader.... Gloves are drawn on.... He steps back, looks at the orchestra, bows to his partner, claps his hands, and – now the music starts up and the dance begins.

But observe this very same company when now the ball is over! It is day; the rays of sun are striking the misted-up windows; the candles in the ballroom are burning as dully and sleepily as many a dancer's so recently sparkling eye. Where is that neatness, that trimness, that decorum of the evening before? The gentlemen's clothes are dusty, their hair tousled, their shirt-frills creased; the cravat falls loosely from under the chin, the bow is askew. And the ladies – the once so festively adorned, so elegant ladies? The dress is no longer white, the cheeks no longer red. The delightful ringlets have lost their elasticity, and hang carelessly down over the bosom – which gleamed last night like marble or alabaster, but today like a wall in need of whitewash. Here a flounce, here a frill has been torn; here a ribbon is missing, here a pin. And then the sweet faces? Alas, the eyes have lost their brightness, the lips their smile and the cheeks their delicate blush; pale, dull and indolent (if I may be permitted to use such an expression), the ladies seem to have sated themselves with the ephemeral pleasures of youth and become experienced, staid and rather sullen matrons within a single night.

But my sweet Maren? Had she not suffered the same heart-sickening transformation? Indeed, indeed – as any other human being she was subject to change, but not a heart-sickening change. The barely perceptible weariness and slight disarray simply gave her a more languorous air; and I need only say that it was on this very same morning that in a fit of tempestuous admiration I wrote one of my most successful poems: 'To Maren, the Morning after the Wedding.'

THE DUCK-SHOOT

It took me a long time to make up my mind as to the style in which this important and eventful chapter should be written. The subject was worthy of the heroic style, but – to be frank – I find that rather difficult, while I find the purely historical approach rather dry. Moreover, I searched in vain for any predecessors on that swampy path. To be sure, one of our poets once ate roast duck for lunch ... it is still uncertain as to whether it was tame or wild – the latter, I presume ... and went around in gumboots, but all that doesn't amount to a duck-shoot. In short, my sources consisted entirely of oral tradition coupled with my own brief experience, and so I shall have to draw on these as best I can.

The noonday sun was already shining on the lake at Svirum Manor when, well-booted and well-armed, we huntsmen gathered together and attempted to harden and brace ourselves against the influence of the water with the help of a hearty lunch (*déjeûner dinatoire*). The meal was enlivened with homemade Danish whisky and spiced with interesting yarns about former exploits, each huntsman trying to surpass the other in daring stories. I, a complete novice, felt quite out of this. Unfortunately I didn't reap the full benefit of such instructive conversation, since many of the expressions and phrases seemed to me puzzling or obscure. Later – so as not to reveal my ignorance – I secretly learned the meaning of these from my friend, young Ruricolus.

At last we set off. Our host, Counsellor Svirum, was in charge, and stationed us at our posts. In order to enable us to see and shoot the ducks as they were chased by the dogs, passages or small clearings had been cut in the reeds and rushes, which stretched from the land right out to the open waters of the lake. I was stationed at the end of such a passage – in fact the last one. Before the boss left me there he gave me several gentle and fatherly warnings.

'I hear, my young friend', he whispered, 'that you know how to handle a gun, though you haven't yet had much experience of hunting. Duck-shooting, dear boy, is a dangerous sport – take care not to shoot except out here in the clearing. And watch out for us in the boat when we get in your line of fire. And for God's sake, don't shoot any of the dogs!'

I promised by everything that was holy, in my usual tone of voice.

'Sh, sh!' he said softly though a little testily, gesticulating with his hand. 'Don't speak loudly at your post!' At this he hurried away, and made for the punt that lay at the other end of the lake. For a good quarter of an hour there was silence.

The weather was fine: the sun shone warmly and the air was clear and still; the lake was as smooth as a mirror. Once in a while a fish jumped, briefly stirring up the shiny surface, whereby the delightful reflection of Svirum Manor, the farm buildings and the trees in the garden was spoilt for me and I myself was roused from my sweet fancies. Thus – I reflected – also our most beautiful hopes are destroyed; thus our magnificent castles in the air disappear; thus first love, quiescent and pure, is replaced with restless passion. But it's no good being sentimental on a duck-shoot; I tried to banish such unsuitable thoughts and turned all my attention to the business of the day and to the duties I now had to fulfil. Not that I considered them very difficult, for I hadn't yet seen or heard a single duck and was on the point of regarding the entire shoot as simply a manoeuvre – a mockery. I was remarkably mistaken.

I was standing there, greatly inconvenienced by gnats and flies – impudent guests that I scarcely dared to chase away with my hand, not merely on account of the warnings I had just received, but because whenever I moved my arms my immediate neighbour, old Pastor Ruricolus, shook his head disapprovingly at me and hissed a long sibilant, yet muffled 'sh' through his teeth. I stood like that, I'm telling you, almost at the mercy of my enemies, against whom I could scarcely defend myself except by blowing and by moving all my facial muscles, when . . . when the sound of a splash followed by a scream – the most terrible scream I had ever heard in my life – came from the other end of the lake and was echoed by the hills and the buildings and gardens of Svirum Manor.

Suspecting an accident, I cried out in horror: 'Pastor Ruricolus, the counsellor must have fallen into the lake!', to which His Reverence replied with laughter; and knowing this to be an infringement of the hunting code, he attempted in vain to stifle it, until after some while it eventually petered out into titters. With a shake of his head and a wave of his hand, he bade me be silent, at the same time relieving my untimely fears. In such calm weather the other huntsmen must also have heard my childish cry and gloated over it, though with greater restraint. This was my first blunder; but it was not to be the last.

Well, then . . . the scream, or rather the yell, did in fact come from Counsellor Svirum; but it was simply a signal – a kind of trumpet call to indicate that the shoot was now to begin. The splash I had heard came from the dogs, who, eight in number, had plunged into the lake in one go. Shortly afterwards they started baying (at the supper table I had once been so unfortunate as to say that they barked, but Pastor Ruricolus took me seriously to task: 'Hounds, my good fellow, do not bark, they bay' – and I promised never to commit such an offence again). So . . . the dogs bayed – first one, and then several others. The ducks started quacking; some flew up over the reeds and dropped down again; others flew up in the air and circled in wide circles around the lake. The shoot progressed; the dogs came nearer and nearer, likewise our leader in the punt. It was not long before the first shot sounded. The report echoed from the manor, and then rolled like thunder down over the lake until it died away among the distant banks of heather – it was my neighbour who had fired the shot. Soon a second huntsman fired too, and eventually the others; this vigorous shooting went on for over an hour. Meanwhile the punt and the dogs had passed by me, and I wondered greatly why I hadn't had a chance to shoot, since most of the ducks would have had to fly over my clearing. But later this mystery was solved.

Though only a passive onlooker, I nevertheless enjoyed this new and unusual spectacle. Dogs and men, equally keen and eager, were in incessant motion: the former ran around in the reeds and rushes, splashing, panting and baying; the latter fired and loaded, took aim and lowered their guns. But on that day no one surpassed our brave host. He was constantly on the move, rushing from one place to the other wherever his presence was most needed, and firing and shouting at the dogs – for he alone might speak. And to judge from his frequently and eagerly repeated 'Fetch it! Haha! Good boy!' I rightly concluded that his bag was considerable.

At last he regarded the shooting-ground as pretty well cleaned out, and called off the shoot. He landed the punt, and all we huntsmen gathered around our bold admiral, each with his booty – I alone came empty-handed. When he had mustered us all and delivered well-deserved praise – especially to Spy, who had covered himself with glory – he turned to me and said, 'But you haven't fired your gun at all?'

'I haven't had anything to shoot at,' I replied. He shook his head. 'I can assure you', I repeated, 'that I haven't seen anything but some fish that swam past me in the surface of the water – but not a single duck.'

At that there was a roar of laughter, like on Olympus when the lame Hephaestus took the shape of a servant and waited at table. And when they had laughed fit to burst they all assured me that what I in my innocence had taken for fish were ducks, and nothing but. Then we all had a glass of whisky, and thus ended the first act. The scene now changed to another part of the lake.

Here the clearings were so long that it was impossible to shoot from the shore. Our leader, who foresaw everything, had therefore adopted a wise – though for me unfortunate – measure. Midway between the land and the open water two poles had been driven in, and on top of these a broad plank had been nailed; from here the huntsman was now able to cover the whole terrain. One by one the counsellor himself took us out in the punt and stationed us on our respective platforms.

When I had mounted mine, the boss left me, saying with a mischievous smile, 'Watch out for the fish when they come swimming past you, and take great care not to fall in!'

I swallowed the first taunt raw, but to his final warning I retorted somewhat arrogantly, 'Don't worry, sir. I don't feel the least bit giddy.'

What vain conceit! And how soon to be punished! When the dogs gave the alarm, here too I saw some of those creatures which I insisted belonged to the fish family, though the others classified them as birds. I stuck to my own opinion until one of these amphibians sailed right past me, or rather below me, and I had to bow to the truth and admit that it was really a duck, which – with only half its head above water and the rest below – was stealing away from the dogs. This time I was determined to shoot, but before I was ready – in fact as soon as I moved the gun – the duck dived down and disappeared. But it was not long before another glided out of the reeds. So I cocked my gun, took aim, pulled the trigger, and – fell backwards into the lake. It was no deeper than that I could soon get my head and shoulders above water.

At the same moment I heard a familiar voice shouting, 'Well, I'll be jiggered! Who was that who fell into the water?' Another answered, 'That lanky Copenhagener,' and a third, 'Punt the boat along and fish him up!' This was done, and – dripping wet, crestfallen and ashamed – I was put ashore, after which I trudged straight back to the manor without stopping. On landing me, the counsellor – stifling his laughter – expressed regret concerning my accident, and told me to go and see his wife, who would find me some dry clothes. My friend, Hans Mikkel, accompanied me, and after this brief interruption the others went on with the shoot, which for me had now lost all its attraction.

YET ANOTHER COOLING-DOWN

With the help of my friend I soon changed my clothes. But, alas, what a travesty! From the counsellor's wardrobe I acquired a complete outfit: a green woollen coat or jacket, which was both too wide and too short, hung like a flowing robe about my slender body and reached far short of my wrists; a yellow plush waistcoat and matching breeches, which crept up above my knees at every step I took; blue woollen stockings, and a pair of boots that slobbered around my calves. I could no longer recognize myself – nor, alas, could my Maren. And no wonder! – for how hideous in comparison with a fashionable black coat, embroidered silk waistcoat, yellow nankeen trousers and gaiters to match. No, I am not mistaken if I ascribe to this confounded outfit my ensuing misfortune – the total change in the lovely Miss Lammestrup's previously so favourable mood.

Had I so much as known that she whom I adored was in the house, I would indeed have stayed in my lonely room until my clothes were dry. But Fate, relentless Fate, which has now for half a century made me the object of her caprices, had decided otherwise. With a jest on my lips regarding my own comical appearance I entered the parlour, where I expected to find only the lady of the house. But – the room was full of ladies, and my jest was superfluous, for the laughter came by itself. This, however, I would not only have been able to bear but would gladly have participated in, had not she – she before whom I would rather have appeared in a nobler costume – been present. She was the first to step forward; dropping a deep curtsey and addressing me as Counsellor, she enquired how I felt after the hot night and the cold bath. My reader must on no account believe that it was her intention to make fun of me. Far from it – if anything, it was a mask she assumed in order to hide her true feelings; for even through her merry laughter I – and perhaps I alone – heard the unmistakable voice of the heart.

When I had served for a quarter of an hour as the target for the arrows of the mischievous girls' wit, I suddenly had an idea, which my evil genius surely put into my head: I suggested that the young ladies should profit from the fine weather and at the same time be witness to the duck-shoot, which – as we could hear from the regular gunshots – was still at its height. My unfortunate proposal was accepted, and we headed – I headed – for disaster. Closer to the lake and the shooting-ground, in the middle of the meadow, was a hill which I chose as a vantage point. In order to reach this we had to cross over a little brook, which was bridged by a plank, though without any railings. I myself – my friend Hans Mikkel having already returned to his duties on the lake – crossed it without difficulty. But when the ladies were to cross, they were all seized with fright and no one wanted to be the first; one dainty little foot after the other was stretched out onto the plank, and just as hastily withdrawn. They screamed, they laughed, but made not the slightest headway.

Yet again a demon whispered to me: 'Carry them across, and you'll instantly have your beloved in your arms!' My innocent heart leapt with joy. I made my suggestion; it was accepted. And yet, when I crossed over to them and stretched out my longing arms, again no one would be the first to entrust herself to them; each would rather let the other have the honour.

At last the brave Miss Lammestrup came up to me and said with a gracious smile, 'I'll try it, but don't drop me in the water – and remember you've had one bath today already.'

Full of false confidence I assured her that she had nothing to fear, lifted her up and supported her on my arm, while hers lay as light as a feather – or a warm iron – or an electrifying machine – on my neck. I was in ecstacy – I would have liked to walk like that, not only over but through the water, for the rest my life – so I thought, poor fool that I was. Yes indeed. I made a start, but there it was to end. Ah! A thousand curses shall be heaped on the head of that tailor who had made Counsellor Svirum's breeches – for it was those that were too tight over the knees and made me wobble! Do not laugh, dear reader – for your laughter is merciless and sinful. But you, tender reader of the fair sex, should weep – for Peer the Fiddler fell into the brook with his lovely burden!

(Interval)

Would that this brook had been the Lethe! Then neither you, my sensitive reader, nor I would have wept over my black – yes, black misfortune! For there was more mud than water in the brook – it was as dirty as the Styx itself. Ah, once again – why was it not the Lethe?

Do not ask me, compassionate reader, how we got to our feet again – what I said, what she said, how loudly she screamed, how loudly the others screamed, how we got home, and so on – I cannot recall a thing. I heard nothing, saw nothing; I was in a kind of trance, and only when I heard someone cry, 'Counsellor Svirum, now your yellow plush breeches have also come to grief,' did I wake up properly.

At these words I mechanically raised my head from the bed in which I lay. There stood all the huntsmen!

'The Devil take the breeches!' cried Squire Lammestrup. 'It was worse for Maren – do you realize what a sight she was?'

'Is she alive?' I asked anxiously. 'Is she out of danger? And will she forgive me, unhappy wretch that I am?'

'Afterwards', he answered, 'it's easy to laugh. She and the other girls are sitting down there chattering and making fun of certain people who fall over their own feet.'

He said the latter with a malicious grin, but I turned my face to the wall like a dying man, and sighed with the poet:

> All ties between us now are severed;
> Branded for ever I stand,
> And can never cleanse that stain –
> To you and those who value their wits and their life

> I have only this advice to give:
> Let no mortal venture to set foot
> On that hellish plank!
> Let it be removed, the sooner the better!
> There's a curse on it!²

'Well, I'll be jiggered!' whispered His Reverence. 'He's raving, he's gabbling in verse.... You must stay with him, Hans Mikkel, so that the rest of us can go down and get a wee drop!'

The huntsmen all crept out of the room, leaving me to my boundless misery.

Three days afterwards my friend and I were rocking on the waves of the Kattegat.

TWENTY YEARS LATER

To conclude this story of mine I shall now refer to the beginning, where I said that after my trip to Copenhagen I made an excursion to Vendsyssel. Here is what came out of my visit:

I rode on my yellow Norwegian pony from Sundbye towards the scene of those singular adventures of my youth. My legs had not yet grown any shorter, so with the toes of my boots I could easily brush the dew off the grass in the deep wheel-tracks, steadying from time to time the horse's wobbly gait. Thus, partly riding and partly walking, I arrived at old Tyreholm, the birthplace of the lovely Maren Lammestrup, around noon. I rode across the meadow where once that curious battle was fought. The haystacks were still standing as before, but the beautiful amazons were gone – '*Die hübschen Mädchen die bleiben fern – o Traum der Jugend, o goldener Stern!*'³ I asked a man who was working there whether Squire Lammestrup was still living at the manor.

'No', he replied, 'he's been dead for many years; Peer Madsen is living here now.'

I would also have enquired about my dear Maren, but

although – if I remember rightly – the images of twenty-one other girls had obscured hers since those golden times, I was reluctant to hear that she too might be dead and gone. I rode on, taking a long look on passing at the house her presence had once embellished.

I approached Svirum Manor. The lake lay in front of me with its wreath of rushes. My eye sought out the brook – that cursed brook which had engulfed one of my fairest hopes. But lo! My curse had been fulfilled: the plank was not to be seen, probably long since consumed by flames – a much too lenient punishment. The entire meadow had been ploughed up and the brook itself had become a dried-up ditch.

'Does Counsellor Svirum live here?' I asked a passer-by.

'He died many years ago,' was the reply.

Then rejoice, you ducks, I thought, and swim around in the peaceful lake with heads held high! There is no longer any Spy to scent out your secret nests, nor will my clumsy body disturb your gleaming element! I rode on quickly.

I knew from the official yearbook that Hans Mikkel, the friend of my youth, had succeeded his father as pastor; for since he left the capital I had neither heard nor seen anything at all of him – out of sight, out of mind! Whether the old Ruricolus had moved to a different living or had retired, or whether he too might be dead, I had no idea.

When we haven't seen a former friend for a fifth of a century – when so many eventful years, packed with experiences, joyful and sad, have passed since the merry companionship of our youth, then our hearts beat with a strangely joyful uneasiness as the hour of reunion approaches. But we very seldom find what we expect, because we are unprepared for the mighty impact of time. We would like to have the friend as he was, and forget that nothing remains as it is. I still thought of my dear Ruricolus as the handsome, fashionable and elegant student, the darling of the ladies, his comrades' amiable, kind and ever helpful friend – cheerful, though moderate and respectable, a clever theologian and a good judge of literature into the bargain. As regards the latter in particular we had once been inseparable; and I was longing to jump off my horse and throw myself into his arms, exclaiming, '*Es waren schöne Zeiten, Carlos,*'⁴, etc. But – things turned out quite differently.

The first human being I saw when I rode up to the parsonage was a fat, ruddy-cheeked man in a threadbare grey coat, wearing clogs and a shabby low-crowned hat. This person . . . I would have taken him for the pastor's coachman or farm hand had not an enormous meerschaum pipe bowl in his hand suggested a tenant farmer . . . this person was standing in the middle of the dunghill surrounded by chickens, ducks, geese and turkeys, which he appeared to be counting with his forefinger.

'Is the pastor at home?' I asked, lightly raising my hat.

'Eighty-seven, eighty-eight, eighty-nine, ninety . . . That's me,' he said.

I opened my eyes wide, and – only then did I recognize the friend of my youth.

'But, pastor!' I cried, 'surely you know me?'

He got down from the dunghill and walked towards me, though slowly and carefully, so as not to tread on the dear little ducklings.

'H'm,' he grunted, with a quiet smile. 'Well, now I come to think of it . . . '

'So you've quite forgotten your old Pietro?' I cried.

'Why, it's you,' he replied, giving me his hand. 'Now I must confess! Come closer, my dear good friend! Morten, take the stranger's horse. Is it used to being in the stable, or would you prefer it out in the paddock? You'll be staying with us tonight, won't you?'

'I have a mind to stay indoors', I replied, 'while my horse would probably prefer to be outside.'

'That's a pretty little thing', he said, walking round the horse as I dismounted, 'but its forelegs are a trifle splayed. . . . Oh, Morten! Brown Kirsten is rutting again – don't forget to put her to the bull. . . . Well, you're most welcome. . . . Put a halter on this jade, Morten, and put him out in the pig-paddock. And don't forget to ring the big sow, she's rooting in the potato patch – did you hear? . . . Go inside now (I did so) and relax. What would you like first? A tea-punch? What have you been doing all this time? You've aged. . . . Maren, bring us some tea-punch!' He shouted out these latter words through the kitchen door.

That reception drove any kind of poetic eruption back into my somewhat chilled breast, and there was no embrace. Meanwhile one child after the other poked its head in through the kitchen door to see the strange man, and at the same time I saw a couple of faces at the window, which disappeared as soon as I caught sight of them.

'Are they your children, all of them?' I asked. 'How many do you have?'

'One for each finger,' he said, morosely. 'But I don't know what I'm going to do with them. It's bad enough as it is, having to keep them in clothes; but to send any of them away to study would be quite out of the question. What's to become of them?'

Then his wife brought the tea; I paid my respects.

'D'you recognize him?' Ruricolus asked her. 'It's the same fellow who once dipped you in the brook at Svirum Manor.'

Yes, indeed, it was she! But, alas how changed she was too – in face, figure and manner.

'Well, I never,' she said with a forced smile, as she laid the tea-table. 'How nice to see you again . . . it's a long time since we had the honour . . . would you like cream or rum?'

But why should I weary my reader any longer by describing a scene that had such a chilling effect on my hot blood? That is how time can eradicate, subdue and destroy beauty, wit and gaiety; and what might remain unravaged is sure to succumb to pecuniary worries – time's faithful ally.

In a dismal mood, I left my poor rusticated friend early the following day, ruminating on the scarcely edifying and well-worn theme: *Tempora mutantur et nos mutamur in illis* – Times change, and we change with them.

P.t.F.

THE HOSIER AND HIS DAUGHTER

*'The greatest grief on earth, I fear,
That is to lose the one you hold dear.'*

Sometimes, when I have been wandering far out on the great moor with only the brown heather around me and the blue sky above me ... when strolling far from people and the reminders of their activity here below, which are really only molehills that Time or some restless Tamberlaine will one day raze to the ground ... when stepping, lighthearted, on winged feet, as proud of my freedom as a Bedouin whom no house, no narrowly bounded field ties to the spot, but who owns, possesses everything he sees, dwelling nowhere but living where he pleases ... when my far-roving eye has glimpsed a cottage on the horizon, thus rudely interrupted in its airy flight ... then sometimes I came to wish – God forgive me this passing thought, for it was nothing more – that this human dwelling would vanish! For trouble and grief dwell there too, as well as quarrelling and wrangling about what is mine and what is yours. Alas, this happy desert is both mine and yours; it belongs to everyone and to no one.

A certain forester is said to have proposed that the whole of this settlement be developed – that trees be planted on the cottagers' fields and in their levelled villages. I myself have sometimes been struck by the far more inhuman thought: what if this had still been heather-covered moor – the same that has lain here for centuries, undisturbed, ungrubbed by human hand! But, as I have said, I have not meant this seriously. For when – exhausted, weary, and languishing with heat and thirst – I have thought with painful longing of the Arab's tent and coffee-kettle, then I have thanked God that a heather-thatched cottage, however far away, gave promise of shade and refreshment.

I was feeling in such a mood some years ago, on a peaceful, warm September day, far out on that same moor which in an Arabian sense I call my own. Not a breath of wind ruffled the purpling heather; the air was close and made me feel drowsy. The distant hills that bounded the horizon seemed to float like clouds around the vast plain, and to assume the many marvellous shapes of houses, towers, castles, people and animals; though all with hazy, shapeless outlines that fitfully alternated like dream pictures. One moment a cottage was transformed into a church, and that in its turn into a pyramid; here a spire shot up, and there another sank down; a man became a horse, the latter in turn an elephant; here a boat was rocking, and there lay a ship with spread sails.

My eye found delight for a while in contemplating these fantastic forms – a panorama that only the sailor or the desert-dweller has a chance to enjoy – when finally, tired and thirsty, I began to search for a genuine house among the many false ones, longing intensely to exchange all my magnificent fairy castles for just one single human habitation. At length I was successful – I soon discovered a genuine farmhouse without any spires or towers, the outline of which became clearer and sharper the closer I approached, and which, flanked by peat stacks, looked far bigger than it really was.

The people living there were strangers to me. Their clothes were plain, their kitchen utensils simple; but I knew that the moorland dweller would often conceal precious metals in an unpainted box or an insignificant-looking wall-cupboard, and a thick wallet inside a patched coat. So when, on entering, my eyes lighted on an alcove stuffed full of stockings, I presumed quite correctly that this was the home of a prosperous hosier (let it be said in parenthesis that I know of no poor ones).

An elderly, grizzled yet still vigorous man rose from the table and gave me his hand, saying, 'Welcome! Where, by your leave, does the gentleman come from?'

One does not take offence at such a direct and indelicate question. The moorland dweller is just as hospitable, though slightly more inquisitive, than a Scottish laird, and one cannot really blame him for wanting to know who his guest is. When I had told him who I was and where I came from he called his wife, who at once set before me everything the house could provide, and urged me with good-natured courtesy to eat and drink – though my hunger and thirst made all her urging superfluous.

I was in the middle of the meal and in the middle of a political discussion with my host when in came a young and extremely beautiful peasant girl, whom I would undoubtedly have taken for a young lady fleeing in disguise from cruel parents and a repugnant marriage had not her reddened hands and genuine peasant dialect convinced me that no such travesty had taken place. She nodded kindly, cast a hasty glance under the table, left the room, and returned almost immediately with a dish of bread-and-milk which she placed on the floor, saying, 'Perhaps your dog is hungry too, sir.'

I thanked her for her attention, but the latter was entirely directed towards the big, ravenous dog, which made short work of the dish and was now thanking the giver in his own way by rubbing up against her; and when she timidly raised her arm, Chasseur mistook the movement, got up on his hind legs and forced the screaming girl backwards towards the alcove – whereupon I called off the dog and explained to her his good intention. I would not have drawn the reader's attention to such a trivial incident had it not been in order to remark that everything becomes those who are beautiful. For in all that she said or did this peasant girl displayed a natural grace that no one could attribute to coquettishness, unless one would designate an inborn, unconscious instinct as such.

When she had left the room, I asked the man and his wife whether it was their daughter. They replied in the affirmative, adding that she was their only child.

'You won't keep her long,' I said.

'God preserve us! What do you mean by that?' asked the father, but his self-satisfied smirk revealed that he knew quite well what I meant.

'I was thinking', I replied, 'that she will scarcely be short of suitors.'

'H'm,' he growled. 'Suitors there may be in plenty, but if they're worth much, that we'd have to talk about. To come courting with a watch-and-chain and a silver-mounted pipe is not enough; there's more to driving a horse than saying "gee up"! 'Well, well,' he continued, supporting himself with both fists on the table and bending down to look out of the low window, 'that must be one of them coming now – a shepherd boy who's just crawled out of the heather – ho! ho! One of those fellows who run around with a couple of dozen pairs of stockings in a haversack – stupid dog! Proposing to our daughter with two oxen and two-and-a-half cows – let's see what he's up to, the beggar!'

None of these outpourings was addressed to me, but to the newcomer, upon whom he fixed his darkened gaze as the former cut through the heather towards the house. He was still so far away that I had time to ask my host about this young man, and learned that he was the son of their nearest neighbour – who, mind you, lived well over two miles away – and that the father owned only a modest dwelling on which, what's more, he owed the hosier two hundred rix-dollars; that the son had been peddling woollen wares for some years and had finally dared to propose to the lovely Cecil, but had been turned down flat. While I was listening to this story Cecil herself had entered the room, and her anxious gaze, which kept on flitting from her father to the wanderer outside, made me suspect that she did not share the old man's view of the matter.

As soon as the young hosier came in at one door she went out of the other, though not without a swift yet tender and pained glance.

My host turned towards the newcomer, gripped the edge of the table with both hands as if he needed support and answered the young man's 'Peace be with you!' and 'Good-day!' with a terse 'Welcome.'

The latter remained standing a moment, ran his eyes around the room, and then, extracting a pipe from his inner pocket and a tobacco pouch from his back pocket, he knocked his pipe out on the stove beside him and refilled it. All this was done slowly and at a measured pace, while my host remained fixed in the position he had adopted.

The stranger was a very handsome fellow – a true son of our Nordic people, who set to work slowly though with vigour and stamina – fair-haired, with blue eyes and red cheeks, the fine down on his chin as yet untouched by a razor although he had probably already turned twenty. He as a pedlar was dressed in finer clothes than those of an ordinary peasant; and even finer than the rich hosier himself, in a coat and wide trousers, a red–striped waistcoat and a blue-flowered cotton kerchief – he was no unworthy suitor for the fair Cecilia. Furthermore, he impressed me with his gentle and open countenance, which bore witness of honesty, patience and endurance – a distinctive feature of the Jutland character.

It was quite a while before either of them would break the silence. At last my host found his tongue, asking slowly, coldly and indifferently, 'And where are you bound for today, Esben?'

The latter answered, as he struck a light and leisurely pulled at his pipe, 'No farther today, but tomorrow I'm off to Holstein.'

There was again a pause, during which Esben examined the chairs, selected one of them and sat down. Meanwhile the mother and daughter entered; the young pedlar nodded at them with such a calm and unruffled expression that I might have believed he was totally indifferent about the fair Cecilia had I not known that in such a breast love can burn strongly however calm it may seem – that it isn't a flame that flares up and sparkles, but a constant, warming glow. Cecilia sat down with a sigh at the bottom end of the table and began eagerly to knit; with a soft-spoken 'Welcome, Esben!' her mother settled down at the spinning wheel.

'I suppose you're going on business?' the host now asked.

'That may well be,' replied his guest. 'I'm going to try and see how much can be earned down south. But my request today is that you will not be in too much of a hurry to marry Cecil off before I return and we can see what luck I've had.'

Cecil blushed, though continued to stare at her work.

Her mother stopped the spinning wheel with one hand, laid the other in her lap and gazed fixedly at the speaker. But, turning to me, her father said, 'Absence breeds forgetfulness. How can you expect Cecil to wait for you? You may be gone for a long time – you may never come back at all.'

'Then that will be your fault, Michel Krænsen,' Esben retorted. 'But this much I'll say: if you force Cecil to marry another you'll be doing both her and me a great wrong.'

With that he rose, shook hands with the two old people and bid them a curt farewell. To his sweetheart he said in a slightly quieter and softer tone, 'Good-bye, Cecil, and thank you for all your goodness. Think kindly of me – that is, if you may. . . . God be with you! – and with you all. Farewell!'

He turned towards the door, replaced his pipe, tobacco pouch and tinderbox each in its appropriate pocket, picked up his stick, and walked away without so much as looking back.

The old man smiled as before; his wife sighed, and set the spinning wheel going again. But tear after tear trickled down Cecilia's cheeks.

At this point I was greatly tempted to outline the principles that ought to guide parents with regard to their children's marriages. I could have reminded them that wealth is not sufficient for matrimonial happiness, that the heart must have its say; that, above all, wisdom invokes us to pay more regard to integrity, diligence and skill than to money. I could have reproached the father (for the mother seemed at least to be neutral) for his harshness towards his only daughter. But I knew the peasantry only too well to waste words on this matter; I knew that wealth means everything for that class – and – I wonder if it is very different for other classes. Furthermore, I was familiar with the peasant's firmness, which almost amounts to obstinacy, on this point; and that in such controversies with his superiors he would often yield and pretend to adopt their opinion, so that they are tempted to believe they have convinced him and won him over, when he is in fact firmly resolved to go his own way.

Besides, there is yet another consideration that bids me refrain from sticking my finger uninvited between the knife and the wall, between the door and the frame, between the hammer and the anvil: is not wealth nevertheless the most tangible of all the good things on earth – of those, *nota bene*, that according to Epictetus's classification 'are not in our power'? Is not money a sufficient surrogate for all worldly pleasures – an indispensable substitute for food and drink, clothes and shelter, for esteem and friendship, and even to a certain extent for love? And is it not wealth that gives us the most pleasures, the greatest independence – that compensates for the majority of our wants? Is not poverty that rock upon which both friendship and love itself may often be wrecked? 'When poverty comes in at the door, love flies out of the window,' is a common saying. And what do we say when the first intoxication of love has evaporated and the honeymoon is over? Would that Amor and Hymen could be lifelong companions, but they both prefer to ally themselves with Pluto.

After thus viewing the world as it is – perhaps more sensibly than some might expect or others wish from the pen of a novelist – my readers will appreciate my consistency if I do not mix myself up in Esben's and Cecilia's romance; so much the more so because on Esben's part it could be a purely rational speculation that calculated less on the beauty and affections of the daughter than on the father's bulging alcove and heavy wall-cupboard. And although I well knew that pure love is not a purely poetic invention, I realized already at the time that it is more frequently found in books than outside them.

When, therefore, the lovely Cecilia left the room – presumably to give private vent to her feelings in a flood of tears – I merely remarked that it was a pity the young lad was not better situated, because he seemed to be a decent fellow and was fond of the girl. 'If only', I added, he could return home with a purse full of money . . .'

'. . . and it even belonged to him', old Michel added slyly, 'that would indeed be a different matter.'

Once again I wandered out onto my humanly deserted and carefree moors. Far away to one side I could still see Esben and the wisps of smoke curling up from his pipe. That, I thought, is how he gives vent to his sorrow and his love, but what of poor Cecilia? I cast yet another glance back at the wealthy hosier's farmhouse and said to myself that, had it not existed the world would have seen far fewer tears.

Six years elapsed before I visited that part of the moor again. It was a September day, and just as warm and peaceful as the last time. Thirst drove me to look for a house, and it so happened that the hosier's was the nearest. Not until I recognized the good Michel Krænsen's lonely dwelling did I come to think of the fair Cecilia and her sweetheart, and my curiosity to learn what had been the outcome of this moorland idyll impelled me just as strongly as my thirst. In such circumstances I am much inclined to anticipate the real story; I make my conjectures, I imagine how things could and ought to be, and then try to see how far my view of the situation accords with the dictates of fate. Alas, as a rule my guesses are very much at variance with the true course of events – as in this case too. I pictured Esben and Cecilia as man and wife, she with a babe-in-arms, the grandfather with a couple of toddlers on his knee, the young pedlar himself as the active and successful manager of the now expanding stocking trade. But things turned out otherwise.

As I stepped inside I heard a soft female voice singing what at first I took to be a lullaby. But the tone was so melancholy that my high hopes were already dashed to the ground. I stood there listening: the song was a lament about hopeless love. Though simply expressed, it was genuine and moving, but I have only been able to remember the refrain that was repeated at the end of each verse:

> 'The greatest grief on earth, I fear,
> That is to lose the one you hold dear.'

Filled with dark forebodings I opened the living-room door.

A stout middle-aged peasant-woman, who sat carding wool, caught my immediate attention, but it was not she who was singing. The singer had her back to me; she sat rocking back and forth, moving her hands as if she were spinning. The former got up and bade me welcome, but I stepped forwards in order to see the other woman's face.

It was Cecilia – pale, yet still beautiful, I thought, until she looked up at me. Alas, it was madness that shone in her dully gleaming eyes, in the sickly smile on her face. I noticed, too, that she had no spinning wheel, but that the one she imagined herself treading must have been of the same stuff as Macbeth's dagger.

She ceased both her singing and her airy spinning, and asked me eagerly, 'Are you from Holstein? Did you see Esben? Will he be coming soon?'

I realized how things stood, and promptly replied, 'Yes, he won't be staying much longer now; he sends you his greetings.'

'Then I must go out and meet him!' she cried happily, jumping up from her little straw stool and skipping over to the door.

'Wait a minute, Cecil,' said the other woman, putting down her cards. 'Let me come with you.' At this she winked at me, shaking her head – her gesticulation was superfluous.

'Mistress!' she shouted, in the direction of the kitchen door. 'There's someone here. You must come, for we have to go out now.' She ran after the demented girl, who was already out in the yard.

The old woman entered. I didn't recognize her, but presumed, in fact quite correctly, that she must be the unhappy girl's mother. Grief and old age had taken their toll of her too. She didn't remember me from my last visit either, but after a 'Welcome! Please sit down', she asked the usual question: 'Where, by your leave, does the gentleman come from?'

I told her, reminding her at the same time that I had been there some years ago.

'Good gracious!' she cried, clapping her hands. 'Is it you? Please sit down at the table while I get you a bite to eat – you must be thirsty too?' Without waiting for an answer she hurried out into the pantry and returned almost immediately with something to eat and drink.

I was of course eager to learn more about poor Cecilia, but a premonition of something extremely sorrowful curbed my curiosity and prevented me from asking straight out what I both wished and dreaded to hear.

'Is your husband not at home?' was the first thing I said.

'My husband....' she said. 'Our Lord has taken him long ago. Yes, indeed, it will be three years come Michaelmas since I was widowed.... Another slice? Please help yourself, though I know it's only peasant food.'

'No, thank you,' I replied. 'I'm more thirsty than hungry.... So your husband has passed away? That must have been a great loss – have caused you great sorrow....'

'Yes, alas,' she sighed, her eyes filling with tears. 'But that was not all.... Good God! Surely you've seen our daughter?'

'Yes', I replied, 'she seemed a bit strange...'

'... She's quite out of her mind', she cried, bursting into tears. 'We have to employ someone just to look after her, and she can manage little else besides. She's really supposed to do some spinning and knitting, but she makes little headway, because she has to run after the girl about sixteen times a day whenever she starts thinking of Esben...'

'... Where is Esben?' I interrupted.

'In God's Kingdom,' she replied. 'So you haven't heard? Mercy on us, he suffered a miserable death; no one ever knew such wretchedness.... Don't feel too proud. Eat and drink what you like.... Yes, indeed, I have gone through a great deal since you were here last. And these are difficult times; the hosiery trade is a thing of the past, and we have to hire strangers to see to everything.'

Since I felt that her grief over the past coupled with her anxiety about the present was no greater than that she would be able to stand telling me her troubles, I begged her to do so. She willingly complied with my request and gave me an account, which – with the exception of some irrelevant remarks – I shall do my best to repeat in the simple and artless manner of the narrator.

'We and Kjeld Esbensen...' she began, after having drawn a chair up to the table, sat down on it and made ready her knitting, '... have been neighbours ever since I came to the farm. Kjeld's Esben and our Cecil became good friends before anybody realized it. My husband wasn't too happy about it, and I wasn't either, because Esben had very little to his name and his father nothing at all. Still, we thought the girl would have had more sense than to set her cap at such a young lad. He did of course run around with a few stockings and earn a shilling or two, but how far would that go? Then they came courting. My husband turned them down – which was not surprising – and Esben set off for Holstein. We noticed that Cecil was somewhat out of spirits, but we didn't pay any attention. "She's sure to forget him", my husband said, "when the right one comes along." And it was not long before Mads Egelund . . . I don't know if you know him, he lives a few miles from here . . . came courting with a fully paid-up farm and three thousand rix-dollars drawing interest. That was good enough. Michel agreed straightaway, but Cecil – God help us, she said no! Then my husband got angry and told her off. I thought he was a bit too hard, but my poor husband always wanted his own way, and so he and Mads's father went to the pastor and had the banns read. It went well enough the first two Sundays, but when he asked for the third time, "Does anyone know of any impediment?", Cecil stood up and cried out, "I do – the banns have been read three times for Esben and me in Paradise." I tried to hush her, but it was too late. Everyone in the church had heard it and was staring over at our pew – we were all put to shame. I hadn't even got as far as thinking that she might have gone out of her mind; but before the pastor could step down from the pulpit she started rattling off that stuff about Esben and Paradise again, about the wedding dress and the bridal bed, and so on and so forth – none of it made any sense. We had to get her out of the church. Poor Michel told her off, and said she was playing a trick on us. So help me, it was no trick – she was in deadly earnest! Crazy she was, and crazy she still is.'

At this the narrator let fall the stocking she was knitting into her lap, unhooked the ball of wool from her left shoulder, turned it round a few times and inspected it from all angles. But her thoughts were elsewhere; after a few minutes she held the ball to both her eyes, hung it up on its hook again and started clicking her needles rapidly, as if to pick up the thread of her sorrowful tale.

'All she could talk about was that she was dead and had gone to Paradise, where she was to marry Esben as soon as he was dead too, and this she kept up both day and night. My poor Michel realized what it was all about. "It's God's work," he said. "No one can withstand His will." But he took it to heart just the same, and God knows how many hours I myself lay awake in bed weeping while all the others were asleep. Sometimes it seemed to me as if it would have been better if the two young people had got married. "That may be so," said my husband. "But it wasn't to be."

'The first couple of months she was very unruly and we had a difficult time with her. Later she calmed down a bit, said very little, but would often sigh and weep. She wouldn't do any work, because "In Heaven", she said, "every day's a holiday."

'Half a year passed in that manner, and it was almost twice as long since Esben had left for the south, nobody having heard anything of him since, either good or bad. Then one day, just as we were sitting here – my poor Michel, Cecil and I – Esben walked in through the door. He had come straight here without going home first, so he didn't know how things stood with us until he looked at the girl and could see that there was something wrong with her.

' "You're a long time about it," she said. "The bridal bed has been made up for more than a year. But tell me first: are you dead or alive?"

' "Good God, Cecil!" he said. "Surely you can see that I'm alive!"

' "More's the pity", she said, "because then you cannot enter the gate of Paradise. Try to lie down and die as soon as you can, for Mads Egelund is awaiting his chance to get there first."

' "This doesn't look too good," he said. "Michel, Michel, you've done us a great wrong. I'm worth five thousand rix-dollars now – my uncle in Holstein has died unwed, and I'm to inherit him."

' "What are you saying?" said my husband. "It's a pity we didn't know before. But take your time, the girl may get well again."

'Esben shook his head, went over to our daughter and took her hand. "Cecil", he said, "talk sensibly now. We're both of us alive, and if only you'd be reasonable your parents would consent to our getting married."

'But she flung her hands behind her back and cried, "Get thee hence! What have I to do with you? You are a man, and I am an angel of God."

'At this he turned round and began to weep bitterly: "May God forgive you, Michel Krænsen!' he said. 'See what you've done to us two wretched people!"

' "Calm down, now!" said my husband, "things may change for the better. Stay here with us tonight, and let's see what she says tomorrow."

'It was evening and a bad storm broke out with thunder and lightning, the worst I've ever known – as if the world were coming to an end. So Esben made up his mind to spend the night with us, and as soon as the storm had abated and the danger of fire was over he laid down in the parlour. The rest of us went to bed too, but for a long time I could hear through the wall how he sighed and wept; I also think he prayed to God in heaven. Finally I dropped off. Cecil lay asleep in the alcove, right opposite Michel's and mine here.

'It must have been an hour or so past midnight when I woke up. It was calm outside and the moon shone through the window. I lay thinking about all the misery that had befallen us; least of all could I have foreseen what I am going to tell you now:

'I suddenly came to think that it was so peaceful over in Cecil's corner; I couldn't even hear her breathing. Nor did I hear anything from Esben. I had a feeling there was something wrong, so I crept out of my own bed and over to Cecil's. I peeped in, feeling for her with my hand; but she wasn't there. Then I was really uneasy, ran out into the kitchen and lit a candle, and went up with it into the parlour. Oh, merciful God in heaven, what did I see? She was sitting in Esben's bed, with his head resting in her lap. But when I looked more closely, his face was deathly pale, and the sheets were red with blood. I screamed and sank to the floor, but Cecil beckoned me with one hand, patting his cheek with the other. "Hush, hush", she said, "my dearest is sleeping sweetly now. As soon as I have buried his body, the angels will take his soul to Paradise, and there our wedding shall take place with great splendour and rejoicing." Alas, dear God, she had cut his throat – the bloody razor lay on the floor beside the bed!'

At this the unhappy widow covered her face with her hands

and wept bitterly, while horror and pain contorted my breast. At last she regained her self-control and continued as follows:

'There was great sorrow and lamentation both here and at Esben's home, but what is done cannot be undone. When he was brought home on the cart to his parents (they thought he was safe and sound in Holstein) there was so much screaming and shrieking, you would have thought the whole house had fallen down. He was a good man, he had come into much money and wealth, and yet he had to die such a miserable death at his young age – at the hands of his sweetheart too. Poor Michel could never forget it either; he was never the same man again. A couple of months later he took to his bed, and then Our Lord took him from me.

'The very same day he was buried Cecil fell into a deep sleep; in fact she slept for three days and nights on end. When she woke up her sanity had been restored. I was sitting beside her bed, expecting our Lord to call her home; but all at once she heaved a great sigh, turned to look at me, and asked, "What has happened? Where have I been? I have had a strange dream – as if I were in heaven, and Esben was with me. Good God, mother, where is Esben? Haven't you heard from him since he left for Holstein?" I hardly knew what to say. "No", I said, "we haven't had much news of him." She sighed! – "Where is father?" she asked. "Your father is well," I answered "God has taken him unto Himself." Then she wept. "Mother, let me see him," she said. "You cannot do that, child," I answered, "for he is in the ground." "God preserve us," she said. "How long have I been asleep then?" I realized then that she herself didn't know in what state she had been. "If you have woken me, mother", she said again, "you have done me a disservice. I was sleeping so sweetly and had such beautiful dreams; Esben came to visit me every night in shining white garments and a string of red pearls around his neck!"'

At this the old woman sank into her melancholy thoughts again and heaved some deep heartfelt sighs before resuming her story.

'The poor child had gained her reason again, but God knows if she was any better off. She was never happy but always subdued, spoke only when spoken to and busied herself with her work. She was neither ill nor well.

'The people in the neighbourhood soon heard about it, and three months afterwards Mads Egelund came to propose to her for the second time. But she wouldn't have anything to do with him, not on any account. Since he then realized that she didn't like him at all, he became gruff and was bent on making mischief. I and my folk and all those who came here always took great care never to let fall the slightest word about how the deranged girl herself had murdered poor Esben; and she probably thought that he was either dead or had got married down south. But one day, when Mads was here, pressing her to accept him, and she replied that she would rather die than marry him, he said straight out that he was not so keen on marrying someone who had cut her first sweetheart's throat; and with that he told her everything that had happened. I was out in the kitchen and heard something of what he said. I threw down what I had in my hand, ran in and shouted at him, "Mads, Mads, may God forgive you! What are you doing?" But it was too late. She was sitting on the bench as pale as a whitewashed wall and with big staring eyes. "What am I doing?" he said. "I'm saying nothing but the truth; it's better she is told than making a fool of her, and letting her wait all her life for a dead man. Good-bye! I'm much obliged!"

'He went away; but she had a relapse, and I don't suppose she will ever recover her wits in this life. You can see for yourself how she is. Whenever she isn't sleeping she is singing that song she herself made up when Esben left for Holstein, and imagines she is spinning her bridal sheets. In all other respects she is quiet, thank God, and wouldn't harm a fly. But we daren't let her out of our sight just the same. God be merciful unto her and soon call both of us home!'

As she spoke these final words, the unhappy girl entered the room with her companion. 'No', she said, 'there is no sign of him today, but he is sure to come tomorrow. I must make haste, if I'm to be finished with these sheets.' She sat down hurriedly on her little straw stool and, briskly moving her hands and feet, she began to sing her lament again. Each time a long, deeply drawn sigh preceded the refrain, 'The greatest grief on earth, I fear, Is to be parted from him you hold dear.' Then her beautiful pale face would droop down towards her bosom, and her hands and feet would rest a moment; but she quickly sat up again, began to sing another verse, and set her shadow-wheel spinning again.

Filled with melancholy thoughts I wandered homewards; my soul had taken on the colour of the desert. The thought of Cecilia and her dreadful fate kept on running through my mind. In every distant fata morgana I seemed to see the hosier's daughter – how she sat spinning and rocking and flinging out her arms. In the mournful cry of the golden plover, in the monotonous, melancholy trills of the lonely wood lark I heard only the sadly true and deeply felt words of many thousands of wounded hearts:

> *The greatest grief on earth, I fear,*
> *Is to be parted from him you hold dear.*

THE PASTOR OF VEJLBYE

A Crime Story

(From Herredsfoged[1] Erik Sørensen's diary, with two appendices by the Pastor of Aalsøe.)

A.

ERIK SØRENSEN'S DIARY.

In the name of Jesus! So now, by the gracious will of God, and on the initiative of my dear lord and master, I, unworthy that I am, have been promoted district sheriff and judge over these people. May the almighty Judge of all the earth bestow on me His blessing, and grant me wisdom and righteousness with which to administer my difficult office! 'Every man's judgement cometh from the Lord': Proverbs 29:26.

It is not good for man to be alone. Now that I am able to support a wife, I ought really to look about me for a helpmate. The Pastor of Vejlbye's daughter is well spoken of by all who know her. Since the death of her dear mother she has managed the household with good sense and frugality. And since there are no other children apart from her and the student, her brother, she can expect a tidy sum some day, when her old father departs this life.

Morten Bruus from Ingvorstrup was here today, wishing to give me a fat calf. But I recalled the words of Moses: 'Cursed be he that taketh reward.' He is a man who is fond of lawsuits – a great haggler and a great braggart. I will have no dealings with him except when I sit before him in judgement.

I have now taken counsel with God in Heaven, and thereafter with my own heart; and clearly I consider Miss Mette Qvist to be the only woman with whom I would wish to live and die. However, I shall quietly observe her for a little while longer. Appearance is deceitful, and beauty is vain. Nonetheless, she is surely the fairest woman I have seen in all my days.

I find this Morten Bruus a most repugnant person – I myself scarcely know why; but whenever I see him, something comes to my mind, like a bad dream – though so dim and hazy that I cannot even tell whether I have ever dreamt about him. It may be a kind of foreboding. He came here again to offer me a pair of Mohrenkopper[2] – splendid animals, and for a song! But that is precisely what struck me. I know that he has bought them separately for seventy rix-dollars and made a pair of them. He would have let me have them for the same sum, but – matched as they are – they are worth a hundred rix-dollars and cheap at that. Is this not bribery in a sense? He is sure to have yet another lawsuit in mind – I will not have his Mohrenkopper.

Today I went to visit the Pastor of Vejlbye. He is indeed a

worthy and god-fearing man, but authoritative and hot-tempered – he tolerates no opposition, and tightfisted he is too. There was a peasant with him at the time who wanted to have his tithe reduced. The man is a wily rogue, for his tithe cannot be set too high. But Pastor Søren told him off in such a way that not even a dog would have taken a piece of bread from him; and the more he scolded, the angrier he became. Oh well, everyone has his faults, to be sure. He means no harm by it, for immediately afterwards he told his daughter to give the man some bread and cheese and a glass of good ale. She is an extremely courteous and pretty girl. She greeted me in such a friendly and modest fashion that it quite touched my heart, and I was incapable of uttering a word. My farm steward once worked there for three years. I shall question him on the sly about how she treats the servants, and whatever else he may know about her. You often get the most reliable information from your servants.

Good God! My farm steward Rasmus tells me that this Morten Bruus fellow went courting at Vejlbye parsonage not so long ago, but was rejected. The pastor thought well enough of him, for the man is comfortably off; but his daughter would have none of him. Pastor Søren is said to have spoken sharply to her at first; but later, when he saw how opposed she was to the match, he let her have her will. It was not pride on her part – says Rasmus – for she is just as humble as she is good; and she readily admits that her own father is from peasant stock just like Bruus.

Now I know what the Ingvorstrup Mohrenkopper were doing here in Rosmus – they were intended to divert the judge from the straight path of justice. Ole Andersen's peatbog and meadow – that pear was well worth this apple! No, no, my good Morten, you don't know Erik Sørensen! 'Thou shalt not wrest the judgement of thy poor.'

Pastor Søren from Vejlbye was here on a brief visit this morning. He has hired a new coachman – a Niels Bruus, brother of the man at Ingvorstrup. This Niels is reputed to be lazy, and cheeky and cocky besides. The pastor wanted him punished and put in jail, but he lacks the necessary witnesses. I advised him to get rid of the fellow at once, or else to make the best of it until quarter day. At first he answered me somewhat heatedly; but when he heard my grounds he admitted that I was right, and even thanked me for my good advice. He is a hot-tempered man, but not difficult to reason with after he has had time to compose himself. We parted as good friends. Not one word was spoken about Miss Mette.

I have spent a very pleasant day at Vejlbye parsonage. Pastor Søren was not at home when I arrived, but Miss Mette received me most warmly. She was sitting spinning as I entered the room, and it seemed to me that she flushed hotly. It was strange how long it was before I could think of something to talk about. When I am sitting in court I am never at a loss for words; and when I am interrogating some rascal I can think of questions in plenty. But before this pure innocent child I stood as shamefaced as a poultry-thief. Finally, I thought of talking to her about Ole Andersen's lawsuit, about his peatbog and his meadow. I don't know how the conversation happened to switch from meadows to flowers, but then one word led to the other – from roses and violets to daisies – until she took me out into the garden to see her flowers. Thus the time passed until Pastor Søren returned home; and then she went into the kitchen and did not appear again until she brought in the supper. Just as she entered the room, the pastor was saying to me, 'It is surely on time that you as well were to think of entering into holy matrimony.' (We had just been discussing the magnificent wedding that had recently been held at Høgholm manor.) Whereupon Miss Mette blushed blood-red yet again. Her father smirked, and said, 'I can see you have been standing in front of the stove, my daughter!'

I have taken the good man's advice to heart, and it will not be long, God willing, before I go courting at the parsonage. For I consider her father's words to be a subtle hint that he would like to have me as his son-in-law. And his daughter – why did she blush? Surely I dare take that as a good sign?

So the poor man is to keep his peatbog and his meadow; but the rich man is certainly very angry with me. Before the judgment was read he stood staring scornfully at poor Ole Andersen. At the words, 'It is the judgment of this court', he looked around the courtroom, grinning slyly, as if quite sure of winning the case. And sure he was, for I know he had let it be known that 'the blighter was foolish to think he could win.' And yet that is what happened. When he heard the verdict, he screwed up his face, which turned as white as a whitewashed wall. But he controlled himself and, as he went out, he said to his opponent: 'Congratulations on the deal, Ole Andersen! The peat-puddle won't beggar me; the Ingvorstrup oxen will get all the hay they can eat.' But outside I heard him roaring with laughter and, as he rode away, he cracked his whip again and again till it echoed in the woods.

It is hard indeed to be a judge. For each verdict you pronounce you can reckon with yet another enemy. Oh well, so long as we can keep on good terms with our conscience – 'for conscience towards God endure grief!'

Yesterday was the happiest day of my life: I celebrated my betrothal in Vejlbye parsonage. My future father-in-law preached on the text, 'I have given my maid into thy bosom': Genesis 16:5. He spoke very movingly of how he was going to give me his dearest treasure on this earth, and of how I must above all be good to her (that I will, so help me God!). I would never have believed that this grave, even harsh man could be so tender. When he came to the end his eyes were filled with tears, and his lips trembled in the manner of one who is trying hard not to weep. My betrothed cried like a child, especially when he came to speak of her late mother. And when he spoke the words, 'Thy father and thy mother shall forsake thee, and the Lord shall take thee up,' I, too, burst into tears – I was thinking of my own dear parents. God has long ago taken them unto Himself in the everlasting habitations, yet has graciously cared for me, His poor child, ever since.

When we had plighted our troth I received the very first kiss from my sweet betrothed. May God give her happiness! She loves me exceedingly well.

At table the guests made merry. Many of her late mother's family were invited; but on her father's side, none, for he has only a few distant relations living right up at the northernmost point of Jutland. There was food and wine in plenty, and after the meal the dancing went on almost until dawn. The Pastor of Lyngbye, the one from Aalsøe and the one from Hyllested, were also present; the latter became so tipsy that he had to be put to bed. My future father-in-law also drank a great deal, but it never showed, for he is as strong as a giant and could easily drink all the pastors in the district under the table. I could also see that it would have amused him to see me a bit fuddled. But I was on my guard – above all I am not a lover of strong drink.

Our wedding is to take place in six weeks. May God bestow His blessing upon it!

It is most unfortunate that my future father-in-law should have taken this Niels Bruus into his service! He is a rough fellow – a worthy brother to him at Ingvorstrup. He should be given his wages and shown the door, rather than having to soil one's fingers on such a brute. But the good pastor is so hot-tempered and stubborn; and two hard millstones don't grind well together. He insists that Niels should serve his time out, even though it means nothing but daily irritations. The other day he gave him a box on the ear, whereupon the fellow threatened that he would 'most certainly pay him back'. But all this took place in private. I have had him before me and both admonished and threatened him. To this he had as good as nothing to say – there is evil in him. My betrothed has herself implored her father to get rid of him, but he will not hear of it. I dread to think what will happen when she moves to my house, for she spares the old man a great deal of trouble and has such a good way of smoothing things over. She is sure to make a loving wife – 'a fruitful vine by the sides of my house.'

It went badly, and a good thing too, for now Niels himself has run away. My dear father-in-law is beside himself with rage, but I am secretly pleased that he got rid of this evil man like that. True enough, that Bruus fellow may seize his chance to take revenge, but we have law and justice in this country, and justice will prevail.

The pastor had told Niels to dig the garden. When he went out to see to him he was standing indolently, leaning on his spade and cracking some nuts he had picked there – but had done no work at all. The pastor told him off, but he replied curtly that he had not been hired as a gardener. For this he received a couple of slaps in the face, whereupon he flung away his spade and swore rudely in return. Then the old man saw red, seized the spade and dealt him some blows with it – that he should never have done, for a spade is a dangerous weapon in the hands of a strong man, especially when raised in anger. At first the rascal falls to the ground as if dead. But when the pastor grows afraid and lifts him up he jumps over the fence and makes for the woods. That is how my father-in-law himself related this unpleasant story. My betrothed is strangely uneasy about it; she is afraid he is going to take revenge in some way or other – harm the cattle, perhaps even set fire to the farm. With God's help there is no need to fear.

Only three more weeks and I shall be leading my sweet betrothed into my house as my bride. She has already been here and inspected everything both inside and out. She was more than satisfied, and praised our neatness and orderliness. The only thing she regretted was having to leave her father; and he will surely miss her. But I shall do whatever I can to compensate him for his loss. I shall give him something in exchange – he shall have my good Aunt Gertrude. She is a capable woman about the house, and still pretty agile for her age.

My betrothed is indeed an angel; everyone else says so too. I am sure to be a happy man – God alone be praised!

Where can the lad have hidden himself, I wonder? Or perhaps he has fled the country? It is at all events a tiresome story; people are gossiping everywhere – backbiting that originates from Ingvorstrup, I should imagine. It would be terrible if my father-in-law should come to hear of it. If only he had taken my advice. For the wrath of man worketh not the righteousness of God. But I am only a layman, and dare not venture to rebuke a servant of the Word of God; besides, he is so much older than I am. No, I hope all this talk will die away by itself. Tomorrow morning I am going to Vejlbye, and shall be able to tell if he has heard anything of the gossip.

The new bracelets I have received from the goldsmith are very handsome, and should certainly please my dearest Mette – if only they fit her. For I took the measurement hastily and in all secrecy with a blade of grass. The bed will be a credit to my aunt; the fringes are particularly fine.

My dear father-in-law was extremely disheartened and ill at ease – I have never seen him like that before. Alas, some obliging persons have told him the stupid rumour that is now common talk in the neighbourhood. That Bruus fellow is reported to have said that the parson was to bring back his brother 'even if he had to dig him out of the ground.' Maybe he is hiding out at Ingvorstrup – gone he is, and no one has seen or heard anything of him since. My poor betrothed is much too dejected; she is troubled by premonitions and bad dreams.

The Lord have mercy on us all! I am so overcome with terror and distress that I can scarcely hold my pen – it has fallen from my hand over a hundred times. My heart is so oppressed and my mind so plagued by uncertainty that I scarcely know how to begin. It seems to have happened all at once, like a peal of thunder. To me time is out of joint: evening and morning are as one, and the whole ghastly day a sudden flash of lightning that has burnt the proud edifice of my desires and hopes down to the ground. A worthy man of God, my betrothed's father, imprisoned and in chains – and as a murderer and villain! The only one hope I have left is that he may nevertheless be innocent. But alas, that is a mere straw for a drowning man to clutch at. He is under great suspicion – and to think that I, miserable wretch, should be his judge, and his daughter, my affianced bride! Lord, my Saviour, have mercy on us. I can do no more.

It was yesterday, that unhappy day, about half an hour before sunrise, that Morten Bruus came to the house bringing with him the cottager Jens Larsen of Vejlbye together with the shepherd's widow and her daughter *ibidem*. Morten Bruus told me that he strongly suspected the Pastor of Vejlbye of having killed his brother. I replied that I had indeed heard some gossip to that effect, but considered it but foolish and wicked slander, since the pastor himself had ensured me that the fellow had run away. 'Had Niels intended to run away', he said, 'he would be sure to have told me first. But these good people can testify that the facts of the case are quite different, and therefore I ask you, as judge, to interrogate them.' 'Think it over!' I said. 'Think it over, my good Bruus, and you other good people as well, before you accuse an honest pastor and spiritual counsellor of unspotted reputation. If, as I strongly suspect, your accusation be unfounded, you can come to pay dearly for it.' 'Pastor or no pastor', Bruus shouted, 'it is written, 'Thou shalt not kill', and it is also written that the authorities 'beareth not the sword in vain.' We have law and justice in this country, and a murderer cannot escape punishment, were he to have the lord lieutenant himself as his son-in-law.' I pretended not to notice the insinuation, and said, 'Very well, be it as you will! What do you, Kirsten Madsdatter, know of this crime of which Morten Bruus accuses your pastor? Tell me the honest truth, as you would defend it before the judgement seat of almighty God, and as you must later affirm by oath in court.' And she came with the following story – that shortly after noon on the day Niels Bruus is reported to have fled from the parsonage she and her daughter Else had been walking past the parson's garden. As they got halfway along the stone wall skirting the east side of the garden they heard someone calling 'Else!' It was Niels Bruus, who was standing just inside the hazel hedge and bending back the branches in order to offer Else some nuts. She took a handful and asked him what he was doing in there. He replied that the parson had told him to dig the garden, but that he had no intention of taking that seriously – he would much rather pick nuts. At that very moment they heard someone come out of the house, and Niels said, 'Look out, now we shall get a rating!' Immediately afterwards they had heard them quarrelling (see they could not, for the wall was too high and the hedge too thick), the one giving as good as the other. Finally they heard the parson shout, 'I shall beat you, you dog! You shall lie dead at my feet!', whereupon they heard two or three smacks, like someone being slapped in the face. Then Niels had called the parson a hangman's assistant and a scoundrel. To this the parson had answered not a word, but on the other hand they heard two dull thuds, and saw the blade and part of the shaft of a spade appear over the hedge twice; but the height and thickness of the hedge prevented them from seeing who was swinging the spade. After that all was quiet in the garden, but they (the shepherd's widow and her daughter) had felt afraid and strangely uneasy, and gone to tend their cattle in the meadow. The daughter told the same story as her mother. I asked them whether they had seen Niels Bruus come out of the garden, which they both denied, although they had looked back many times.

All this completely tallied with what the pastor had already told me; and it was feasible enough that they had not seen the man come out of the garden, because he was just as close to the woods – for which the pastor said he had made – on its south side.

To Morten Bruus I then declared that the testimony of the witnesses was no proof of the alleged murder, especially since the pastor himself had already told me the whole story of his own free will exactly as the women had recounted it. At this he smiled acidly, and asked me to interrogate the third witness, which I proceeded to do. Jens Larsen declared, that very late one evening (as far as he could remember it was not the evening of the day Niels Bruus had run away, but the following one) he was walking home from Tolstrup along the customary path east of the parsonage garden, when he had heard the sound of someone digging. At first he had felt a bit frightened, but since it was a clear moonlit night he nevertheless decided to see who could be busy in the garden at such a late hour. So he had removed his clogs, scrambled up the wall and made a little peephole through the hedge with his hands. From there he saw the parson in his morning gown with his white cotton nightcap on his head, patting down the earth with a spade. When the parson suddenly turned round, as if sensing someone's presence, the witness had become frightened, had hastily slithered down the wall and just as hastily run home.

Although I certainly found it odd that the pastor could be out so late in the garden, I still did not find anything so unusual as to arouse any suspicion of the alleged murder. This I told his accuser, warning him solemnly that he should not only withdraw his accusation but also publicly declare the rumour to be unfounded and himself disclaim any part in it. To this he retorted, 'Not until I see what the parson has dug down in his garden.' 'By then', I replied, 'it may well be too late, and you will be staking your honour and welfare on a dangerous game.' 'That I owe my brother', he replied, 'and I would not expect our judicial authorities to deny me the aid and support of the law.' Such a challenge I could not dismiss.

So, with the accuser and the witnesses, I set off for Vejlbye in a singularly troubled state of mind – less for fear of finding the fugitive in the garden than from concern about the shock and vexation to which the pastor and my betrothed would thereby be exposed. On my way there I could think of little else than letting the slanderer suffer the full weight of the law. Alas, merciful Heaven, what a cruel discovery awaited me.

I would first have taken the pastor aside in order to forewarn him, thus giving him time to compose and control himself. But Morten Bruus anticipated me. For as I drove into the yard he dashed past me on his horse and straight up to the door; and as the pastor opened it he cried out, 'People are saying that you have killed my brother and dug him down in your garden. I have come here with the sheriff in order to search for him!' This indictment so astonished the pastor that he was unable to utter a word before I jumped out of the carriage and said to him, 'You have now heard the charge, straight and to the point. By virtue of my office I am obliged to comply with this man's request, and your own honour now requires that the truth be brought to light and the slanderers be silenced.' 'It is hard indeed', he replied, 'that a man of my calling should be compelled to refute such a cruel accusation. But enter if you will, my garden and my whole house are open to you.' We entered the house and passed through to the garden, where we encountered my betrothed, who was terrified to see Morten Bruus. 'Don't upset yourself, dearest', I whispered to her hurriedly. 'Go inside, and don't be anxious. Your enemy is heading for his own downfall.'

Morten Bruus led the way eastwards through the garden to the hawthorn hedge, the rest of us following with the pastor's servants, whom he himself had ordered to come with spades and forks. The accuser stood looking around until we caught up with him. Then he pointed to a place on the ground, and said, 'This looks as if it has been dug up fairly recently. Let us search here.' 'Dig!' shouted the pastor, angrily. The men started digging, and Bruus, who thought they were taking too long about it, snatched the spade out of one of the men's hands and eagerly set to work. When they had dug a couple of spits deep the ground was so hard that one could clearly see it had not been dug up recently – perhaps not for many years. We all rejoiced – all except one – and the pastor most of all; he had already begun to triumph over his accuser. 'Did you find anything, you slanderer?' he mocked. The latter did not reply; but having pondered a moment, he shouted, 'Jens Larsen, where was it you saw the parson digging?' While the digging had been going on Jens Larsen had been standing with clasped hands watching the work. At Bruus's words he woke up as if from a dream, looked around him, and then pointed over towards a corner of the area about six to eight yards from where we were standing. 'I think it was over there,' he said. 'What is it you're saying?' shouted the pastor, angrily. 'When have I been digging?' Without taking any notice, Morten Bruus called the men over to the spot indicated. He cleared away some withered cabbage stalks, branches and other refuse that was lying there, and the digging was resumed.

I was standing quite calmly and well-satisfied, talking to the pastor about the case and the punishment for which the accuser had made himself viable, when one of the men shouted, 'For Christ's sake!' We looked in that direction – the crown of a hat had become visible. 'Here we'll probably find what we are looking for!' cried Bruus. 'It's Niels's hat. I know it well.'

It was as if all my blood froze to ice; all my hopes were dashed to the ground with a single blow. 'Dig! Dig!' shouted the dreadful blood-avenger, as he himself dug for dear life. I glanced at the pastor; he was as pale as a corpse, but his eyes were wide open, staring fixedly at that ghastly spot. Again a scream! A hand seemed to stretch up out of the ground towards the diggers. 'Look!' shouted Bruus. 'He's reaching out for me. Wait a bit, brother Niels, revenge you shall have.' Soon the whole body was dug out – it was indeed the missing man. His face was hardly recognizable, since it had begun to decay and in addition the nose was crushed and flattened. But all his clothes, right down to the shirt with Niels's name sewn on it, were immediately recognized by all his fellow servants. And the men standing around even recognized a leaden ring in the left ear as the one Niels Bruus had worn constantly for several years.

'Well, parson', shouted Morten Bruus, 'come and lay your hand on the dead[3], if you dare!' 'Almighty God', sighed the pastor, raising his eyes to Heaven. 'Thou art my witness that I am innocent. Strike him I did, but no worse than that he could run away. Strike him I did, and that I now bitterly repent. But as to who has buried him here, only Thou, the Omniscient, knoweth.' 'Jens Larsen knows it too!' shouted that Bruus fellow, 'and there may be others besides. You, honourable judge, will presumably be interrogating his servants, but first I expect you to place this wolf in sheep's clothing in safe custody.'

My God, I dared no longer have any doubt, for the case was all too obvious – but I was ready to sink into the ground from terror and loathing. I was just about to tell the pastor that he should make ready to go to jail when he himself addressed me – he was pale and trembling like an aspen leaf. 'Appearances are against me', he said, 'for this is the work of the Devil and his angels. But there remains yet One who will surely bring my innocence to light – come, Sheriff, I shall await, chained and bound, the fate He has decided for me, poor sinner that I am. Comfort my daughter, and remember that she is your betrothed.' Scarcely had he said this when behind me I heard a cry and the sound of someone falling – it was my betrothed. She lay there on the ground in a faint – would to God that we had both of us lain there, never to wake again! I lifted her up and held her in my arms, thinking she was dead, but the pastor tore her away from me and carried her inside. And just at that moment I was called over to the slain man again in order to inspect a wound in his head, which was not very deep but had cracked open his skull, and had obviously been caused by a spade or some other blunt instrument.

After this we all went into the house. My betrothed had come to herself again. She flung her arms around my neck and beseeched me in the name of God and all that was sacred to save her father from this great misfortune, and thereafter begged me, for the sake of our love, to allow her to accompany him to prison, which request I granted. I myself accompanied them to Grennaae jail, but in God knows what state of mind. None of us spoke a word during the entire sorrowful journey. I parted from them with a broken heart.

The body has been laid in a coffin that Jens Larsen had been keeping for himself, and tomorrow it will be decently buried in Vejlbye churchyard.

Tomorrow the evidence will be presented in court for the first time. God give me strength, miserable creature that I am!

Would to God I had never been appointed to that sorrowful office, which, fool that I am, I so eagerly coveted! It is a hard job to be a judge – would that I could change places with one of the jurymen! When this servant of the Word appeared before me in court, chained from hand to foot, I came to think of Our Lord as he stood before the judgement seat of Pontius Pilate. And it seemed to me as if my betrothed in person – alas, she is lying ill in Grennaae – whispered to me, 'Have nothing to do with that just man.' Aye, would to God that he was, but I cannot yet perceive the slightest possibility. When interrogated, the first three witnesses reaffirmed on oath their entire statement, word for word. Nothing was retracted, nothing added. And besides these, three new witnesses appeared: the pastor's two farm hands and the milkmaid. On the day the murder had taken place the two former had been sitting in the servants' room, and through the open window they had distinctly heard the parson and the slain man quarrelling violently, and heard the former say – in the very words of the shepherd's widow and her daughter – 'I shall beat you, you dog! You shall lie dead at my feet!' In addition they had heard the parson threaten and abuse Niels Bruus twice. They testified furthermore that if the parson was angry he did not hesitate to hit people with whatever was at hand, and thus he had even hit his former boy with a maul. The milkmaid declared that on the same night that Jens Larsen had seen the parson in the garden she had been lying awake unable to sleep, and had heard the door leading from the passage out into the garden creak; and when she got up and looked outside she had seen the parson in his morning gown and nightcap go out into the garden. What he was doing there she had not seen, but about an hour later she heard the garden door creak once more.

When the witnesses had been interrogated, and I asked the unfortunate man if he wished to confess to the crime, or – if not – whether he had anything to say in his own defence, he clasped his hands in front of him and said, 'So help me God and His Holy Book, I shall speak the truth, and I am convinced of nothing other than what I have already confessed. I did strike the deceased with the spade, but no harder than that he could run away from me afterwards, and out of the garden. What has happened to him since, or how he has come to lie buried in my garden, I do not know. As to the testimony of Jens Larsen and the milkmaid, that they had seen me in the garden at night, either they are lying or it is a Devil's delusion. I, unhappy man, have no one to defend me here on earth – that I can clearly see. If God in Heaven chooses to remain silent, then I must submit to His inscrutable will.' Whereupon he bowed his head, let his arms fall and uttered a deep sigh.

Many of those present could not refrain from weeping. People started murmuring softly that he might perhaps be innocent; but this was merely the outcome of sympathy and compassion. My own heart, too, burned to acquit him. But emotion must on no account prevail over a judge's good sense; neither pity nor hate, neither gain nor malice, must be allowed to tip the scales of justice. Try as I will, I cannot come to any other conclusion than that the accused has slain Niels Bruus, though scarcely with deliberate intent or purpose. I know full well that he had been in the habit of threatening those with whom he was angry, that he 'would remember them one day when they least expected it', but I have never known him to carry out his threats. Of course every man wishes to save his own skin, if he can, and to vindicate his honour, and that is why he persists in his denials as long as he is able.

Morten Bruus . . . he's a rough customer, and his indignation over the murder of his brother has made him even worse than ever . . . began to speak of instruments that could force an obdurate sinner to confess. But God forbid that I should put such a man on the rack! Anyway, what is the rack other than a trial of physical and mental strength or weakness? Both he who can withstand torture and he who succumbs to it – they may both be lying. A forced confession can never be reliable – no, I would rather resign my seat on the bench and lay down my irksome office.

Alas, my good and gentle betrothed! She is lost to me as far as this world is concerned, and yet I loved her so dearly.

I have had a painful encounter. As I sat pondering on this terrible case, in which I am to be the judge, the door bursts open and the pastor's daughter ... I dare scarcely call her my betrothed when she may never become my wife ... she rushes in with her hair streaming down her back, throws herself at my feet and embraces my knees. I lifted her into my arms, and it was some while before either of us could speak for our tears. I was the first to control my great grief, and said, 'I know what you want, dear heart – you wish me to save your father? May God help us poor mortals, for I myself cannot. Tell me, dear child, do you believe your father to be innocent?' She put her hands to her bosom, and said, 'I do not know,' and then she began to weep again most bitterly. 'That he buried him is most unlikely', she went on to say, 'but that the fellow has died out in the woods from the blows he received – alas, that must be so.' 'My dear', I said, 'but Jens Larsen and the milkmaid saw him in the passage that night.' She shook her head slowly and replied, 'The Evil One can have pulled the wool over their eyes.' 'Lord Jesus forbid that he should have such power over Christian folk,' I replied. She started to weep again. 'Tell me honestly', she began after a moment, 'tell me frankly, my betrothed, if God does not throw a different light on this case, what verdict will you pronounce?' She was looking at me anxiously, her lips trembling. 'If I wasn't convinced that any other judge would be more severe than I was', I replied, 'I would resign my seat on the bench – aye, gladly lay down my office. But since you ask me, this I dare not conceal: the mildest sentence decreed by both God and the King is "life for life".' At this she sank to her knees, though rose to her feet again almost immediately and, stepping back a few paces, cried as if in bewilderment, 'Will you murder my father? Will you murder your betrothed? Can you see this?' – she advanced towards me again, holding out in front of me her hand with the ring on it –

'Can you see this betrothal ring? What did my unhappy father say that time you placed it on my finger – that he would give me "into thy bosom"? But you . . . you pierce my bosom!' Dear God, every word she said pierced my own. 'Dearest child', I sighed, 'do not say such things. You're torturing my heart with glowing tongs. What will you have me do? Acquit a man whom the laws of God and mankind condemn?' She became silent, and gazed into space. 'There is one thing I will do', I continued, 'and if it be wrong, may the Lord not hold this sin against me. Listen, dear child, if this case is pursued to the end, then his life will be forfeited. I can see no way of saving him other than flight. If you can devise any plan of escape, I will close my eyes and remain silent. But listen, as soon as your father was imprisoned I made haste to write to your brother in Copenhagen, and we can expect him any day now. Have a talk with him, and try to make friends with the jailer; if you are short of money, all that I possess is yours.' No sooner had I said this than her face flushed all over with joy, and she threw her arms around my neck, crying, 'May God reward you for this advice! If only my brother were here, we could think up a plan.' 'But where should we go?' she continued, letting go of me. 'And if we were to find a refuge in some foreign land I should never see you again.' She sounded so pitiful that my heart was fit to burst. 'My dearest love', I cried, 'I shall find you no matter how far you travel. And should our means be insufficient for our livelihood, these hands of mine shall work for us all – in my youth I learned how to use an axe and a plane.' Once more she was overjoyed, and kissed me again and again. We both prayed to God with all our heart that He would see fit to further our plan, and she parted from me with renewed confidence.

I too began to hope for the best. But no sooner had she gone than my mind was filled with a thousand doubts, and all the difficulties I had previously thought possible to overcome now seemed like huge mountains that my weak hands would never be able to move. No, no – out of this miserable darkness only He for whom the night shineth as the day knows the way.

Again two new witnesses! They cannot have anything good up their sleeves, because Bruus announced them with an air for which I did not care – he has a heart as hard as stone, and full of venom and gall. Tomorrow they are to appear in court. I am as uneasy as if they were to testify against me myself. May God give me strength!

It is all over – he has confessed everything.

The court was in session, and the prisoner was brought in to hear the testimony of the new witnesses. They declared that on the night in question they had been walking along the road that runs half-way between the wood and the pastor's garden when they saw a man with a sack slung over his shoulder emerge from the wood and walk past them in the direction of the garden. They could not see his face, for it was hidden by the sack, but in the moonlight they could clearly see that he was wearing a loose-fitting green robe (his morning gown, in fact) and a white nightcap. The said person disappeared at the garden fence.

No sooner had the first witness given evidence than the pastor's face turned an ashen grey, and it was all that he could do to utter softly the words, 'I feel ill.' He was given a chair, and that Bruus fellow turned to the people next to him and said, 'That jogged the parson's memory, didn't it!' The pastor did not hear this, but beckoned to me and said, 'Let me be taken back to my cell; I wish to talk to you there.' His request was granted. We drove off to Grennaae jail, the pastor riding in the wagon with the jailer and the constable, I on horseback. When the door of the cell was opened, my betrothed was standing there, making her father's bed; on a chair by the head of the bed hung the incriminating green morning gown. My betrothed uttered a cry of joy when she saw me appear; she imagined my father had been acquitted and that I myself would now escort him from jail. She dropped what she had in her hands and flung her arms around his neck. The old man wept as if he would never cease. He hadn't the heart to tell her what had just taken place in court, but sent her on some errands in town – she was to purchase various things. Before she left she ran over to me, pressed my hand to her bosom and whispered, 'Good tidings?' To conceal my pain and confusion I kissed her on her brow and said, 'Dearest, you shall hear what has happened later – I don't yet know if it makes any difference – but go now, and fetch what your father has asked for.' She departed. Alas, what a pitiful change, out here in this dismal jail with this grief and pain, this constant fear and trembling, from the time when this innocent child dwelt, carefree and happy, in the cheerful parsonage.

'Be seated, my friend,' he said, sitting down himself on the edge of the bed. He folded his hands in his lap and stared down at the floor for a while, deep in thought. Finally, he sat up straight and fastened his eyes on me. I waited in anxious silence, as if I was to hear my own sentence – indeed in a sense I was. 'I am a great sinner,' he began. 'God knows how great – I myself do not. He will punish me here on earth, so that I may receive grace and blessedness in the hereafter. Praise and glory be unto Him!' At this point he seemed to gain more strength and equanimity, and proceeded as follows:

'Right from childhood, as long as I can remember, I have always been quarrelsome, hasty and proud, unable to stand any opposition but always ready to resort to blows. However, I have seldom let the sun go down on my wrath, nor have I borne malice towards any man. When I was still only a boy I did something in a fit of temper, which I have often deeply regretted and which still pains me every time I think of it. Our watchdog, a gentle animal that had never harmed any living creature, had grabbed a sandwich I had put down on a chair. In my rage, I kicked the dog so hard with my clog that it died in agony, yelping miserably. It was only a dumb animal, and yet it was a foreboding that I might come to lay violent hands on my fellow men. When travelling abroad as a student, I picked a quarrel with a German student in Leipzig, challenged him to a duel, and wounded him in the chest so severely that he only narrowly escaped death. Already then I deserved what I must suffer so much later, but now the punishment falls with tenfold weight upon my sinful head – an old man – pastor, messenger of peace – and father. Alas, my God! Alas, my God, this last is the deepest wound of all. . . .' He jumped up, wringing his hands until the joints cracked. I would have said something to comfort him, but could not find words.

When he had composed himself a little he sat down again, and continued: 'To you, formerly my friend and now my judge, I shall now confess to a crime that I have beyond any doubt committed, but of which I am not fully conscious. . . .' – I started in surprise, not knowing what he was getting at nor whether he knew what he was saying, for I had been prepared for a full and open confession – '. . . Don't misapprehend me, but pay attention to what I am saying. That I struck the wretched fellow with the spade, I know and have openly confessed – whether with the flat side or with the edge I was too greatly exasperated to notice. That he then fell down, and ran away – look, that is all I know with certainty. The remainder – namely, that I fetched the body and buried it – has been related, alas, by the four witnesses, and I am compelled to believe it must actually be so. You shall hear my reasons.

'It has happened three or four times previously in my life that I have walked in my sleep. The last occurrence – it must be nine or ten years ago – took place when I was to preach a funeral sermon the following day over a man who had met with a sudden and painful death. I was at a loss for a text, when the wise words of one of the ancient Greeks came into my head: "Call no man happy till he dies." To make use of a heathen text in a Christian sermon would never do, but it came to my mind that the same thought, expressed in almost the same words, was to be found somewhere in the Holy Bible. I searched and searched, but couldn't find the place. It was late, and I was already tired from other work, so I undressed and went to bed, and soon fell asleep. When I woke the following morning and sat down at my desk in order to choose a different text and prepare my sermon, in front of me on the table, written in large letters on a piece of paper, I saw to my great astonishment the words: "Call no man happy before his death: Ecclesiasticus, Chapter XI, verse 34" – but not only that, a funeral sermon as well – brief, yet as well-written as any – and all this in my own handwriting. No one had been in the room; I had bolted the door on the inside, because the lock was worn and the door could have burst open by itself in the wind. No one could have entered by the window, because it was winter and the frame had frozen fast to the window ledge. Now I knew who had written the sermon – none other than I myself. And this was only six months after I had entered the church at night in this selfsame state, and had fetched a handkerchief I distinctly remember having left on my chair behind the altar in the evening.

'Do you understand now, dear friend? When the two witnesses testified in court today, I suddenly came to think of this sleepwalking of mine. And I remembered as well that the morning after the body was buried I had been surprised to find my morning gown lying on the floor just inside the door, because every evening I usually hang it over a chair beside my bed, which fact had escaped my memory until that moment. The unfortunate victim of my uncontrollable rage must have dropped down dead in the woods, then, and I have seen this, as if in a dream, and gone to look for him there. Oh, God have mercy on me – it must be so.'

He stopped speaking, covered his face with his hands and

wept bitterly. But I was utterly astonished and full of misgivings. I had always imagined that the victim had fallen dead on the spot and been buried where he fell – even though it seemed strange to me that the pastor should have carried out this task in broad daylight without anyone noticing it, and that he should have had sufficient presence of mind to do so. But – I had a second thought – necessity must have forced his hand; he has hurriedly covered over the body and dug it down deeper later that night. But now the last two witnesses say that they saw him carrying a sack from the woods. This struck me at once as most extraordinary, and the thought passed through my mind that this testimony might conflict with the previous statements and that the man's innocence might thus be brought to light. But no, alas, it all fits together only too well and he is guilty beyond doubt. Solely the curious twist he gives the case still perplexes me. That he has done the deed is certain, but whether the last and less important half of the crime was carried out while awake or dreaming remains the only mystery. The pastor's statements from first to last, his whole bearing, bears the hallmark of truth; indeed, for the sake of truth he is willing to sacrifice his life. He may, however, be struggling to preserve a modicum of honour, or – this too may be the truth? Such incidents of sleepwalking are not without precedence, nor is it impossible for a man with a mortal wound to run so far.

He paced up and down the room again a few times, then stopped in front of me. 'Here between the walls of this prison you have now received my full confession,' he said. 'I know that your lips will be forced to condemn me, but what does your heart say?' 'My heart', I replied – I felt so oppressed that I could scarcely utter a word – 'my heart suffers unspeakably, and would at this moment most willingly break, if it could thereby save you from a terrible and shameful death . . .' (the last resort, flight, I dared not even mention) 'That you cannot do,' he hastily cut in, 'my life is forfeited, my death is just, and a warning to all coming generations. But promise me that you will not desert my poor daughter. I had hoped, once, to give her to you in holy wedlock . . .' (here he paused to dry the tears that welled up in his eyes again) '... but this sanguine hope I have myself destroyed. You cannot wed the daughter of a malefactor, but promise me that you will provide for her – like another father.' With great anguish and many tears, I gave him my hand. 'I suppose you have heard nothing from my son of late?' he continued. 'I hope that he may remain ignorant of this wretched affair until everything is over – I could not bear to see him.' At this he buried his head in his hands, turned round and rested his forehead against the wall, sobbing like a child.

It was some while before he was able to speak. 'Leave me now, my friend', he said at length, 'and let us not see one another again until we meet in that house of stern justice. And now – show me this last act of friendship: let it be soon – tomorrow, even. I long for death; for I hope, God willing, it will mean for me the start of a better life than this on earth, which has nothing else to offer me now but anguish and dismay. Go now, my dear compassionate judge – let me be brought to the court tomorrow. And send today for Pastor Jens in Aalsøe, he shall prepare me for death – may God be with you!' He gave me his hand, averting his face; I stumbled out of the prison – I was as if numbed, indeed scarcely conscious.

I should perhaps have ridden straight home without speaking to his daughter, had she not herself come to meet me just outside the prison. She must have been able to read the death sentence on my face, for she paled and seized both my arms. She looked at me as if begging for her life. Ask she could not, or else she didn't dare. 'Flee, flee – and save your father!' was the only thing I managed to say.

I threw myself onto my horse, and was home long before I knew it. So be it – tomorrow!

The judgment has been pronounced. He heard it with greater fortitude than he who pronounced it. All those present, with the exception of his stubborn enemy, displayed great compassion. Some even whispered that it was severe – aye, severe indeed, for it deprives one man of his life and three others of their happiness and peace of mind. May the merciful God judge me more leniently than I, poor sinner, dare judge my fellow men.

She has been here – she found me sick in bed – there is no longer any hope – he refuses to flee.

The jailer had been won over. The fisherman, a cousin of her late mother, had promised to sail them to Sweden, and have his sailing boat in readiness; but the penitent sinner was not to be persuaded. He does not wish to evade the sword of justice, hoping that through his and our Saviour's death he will find salvation in the hereafter.

She left me just as inconsolable as when she came, but without a single reproach. God be with her, poor child! How will she endure the terrible day? And here am I, sick in body and in soul, and can neither comfort nor help her – the son stays away.

Farewell, farewell, affianced bride of my heart! Farewell in this miserable world until we meet again in a better one.

Soon, perhaps. For I feel that Death has me in his grasp – perhaps I shall go thither before the one whom my cruel office has forced me to dispatch.

'Farewell, my dearest!' she said to me. 'I leave you without bitterness, for you did only your stern duty. But now I bid you farewell, for we shall never meet again.' She made the sign of peace over me – though I would that God will soon grant me eternal peace!

Merciful God, where will she go? What does she intend to do? Her brother has not come – and tomorrow – at Ravnhøj.*

---

* The mound on Aalsøe meadow outside Grennaae, where pastor Søren Qvist was beheaded, is still known as Ravnhøj [Raven's Hill].

(Here Judge Erik Sørensen's journal comes to an abrupt end. But for the further elucidation and completion of this terrible yet nonetheless true tragedy,

B.

THE PASTOR OF AALSØE'S ACCOUNT

In the seventeenth year of my office an event occurred in this neighbourhood which struck everyone with terror and dismay and reflected shame and disgrace upon our cloth; for the Pastor of Vejlbye, the erudite Søren Qvist, killed his servant in a fit of rage and thereafter buried him at night in his garden. After the preliminary investigation in court he was convicted of having committed this cruel deed, both on the strength of the testimony of many witnesses and of his own confession, and was thereupon sentenced to be beheaded. This sentence was carried out here on Aalsøe Common in the presence of many thousand spectators.

The condemned man, whose spiritual counsellor I had formerly been, sent for me to visit him in jail, and I can truthfully say that I have never administered the holy sacrament to a more well-prepared, repentant and believing Christian. He himself admitted with deep contrition that he had walked after the flesh and been a child of wrath, for which reason God had abandoned him to sin and hardheartedness, humbled him deeply and made him most wretched, so that he could raised up again by the Lord Jesus. He maintained his composure right to the end, and on the place of execution he delivered to those assembled a speech full of force and unction, which he had composed during his last days in confinement and learnt by heart. Its subject was anger and its terrible consequences,

---

his neighbour and colleague, the Pastor of Aalsøe, has appendaged his written account. Should any reader nevertheless doubt the authenticity of these documents, though he may question the actual wording he cannot reject the essence of the story, which, alas, is all too true. The story, which is still talked about in the entire district to this very day, has a sequel: it is precisely as a consequence of this tragic event that ever since then criminal cases have been tried in all the courts. Legal experts should be able to determine the date thereof.)

with touching reference to himself and to the cruel misdeed to which anger had induced him. His text was taken from the Lamentations of Jeremiah, Chapter II, verse 6: 'The Lord hath despised in the indignation of His anger the priest.' When finished, he disrobed, then bandaged his own eyes and knelt down with folded hands. And as I said the words, 'Be comforted, dear brother! Today shalt thou be with the Saviour in paradise,' the executioner's sword severed his head from his body.

That which made death bitter to him was the thought of his two children, the elder of whom, a son, was absent, as we believed, in Copenhagen – but as we later ascertained, in the Swedish town of Lund, from whence he did not arrive until the evening of the same day on which his father had paid the wages of sin. Feeling compassionate towards the daughter – who, to the even greater heart-ache of herself and her betrothed, had for a short while been affianced to the judge – I had her brought to my home, where she arrived early in the morning, more dead than alive, after having taken leave of her father, whom she had tended in prison with filial affection.

When I returned home from the most mournful walk of my life I found her fairly calm, and busy preparing her father's shroud (for she had been permitted, though in strict privacy, to bury her father in consecrated ground). She no longer wept, but nor did she say anything. I too was silent, for what could I say to her? And was not I myself weighed down by dark thoughts?

About an hour later my cart arrived with the body, and shortly afterwards a young man on horseback rushed into the yard – it was the son. He threw himself upon his father's dead body, and thereafter into his sister's arms. The brother and sister held each other in a long embrace, but neither of them could utter a word.

In the afternoon I had a grave dug just outside the porch of Aalsøe church, and there, at the quiet hour of midnight, the earthly remains of the former Pastor of Vejlbye were interred. A tombstone with a cross chiselled on it, which had originally been prepared for myself, covers the grave, and reminds every churchgoer of this unfortunate man's deep fall, of the depravation of human nature and the sinner's only salvation through the Cross of Christ.*

Next morning both of the fatherless children had disappeared, and no one has been able to trace them since. God alone knows in which nook or cranny they had hidden themselves from the world.

The judge is constantly ailing, and is not expected to live. I myself am greatly afflicted with grief and distress, and feel that death must altogether be the greatest blessing for us all.

May God do unto us according to His wisdom and mercy.

Lord, how inscrutable are Thy ways!

In the thirty-eighth year of my office, and twenty-one years

---

* The tombstone is still lying in the same place this very day.

after my colleague and neighbour, Pastor Søren Qvist of Vejlbye, had been charged, sentenced and executed for the murder of one of his servants, a tramp turned up here at the parsonage. He was an elderly man with grizzled hair, and walked with a crutch. None of the domestics was there at the time, so I went out into the kitchen myself to give him a piece of bread, and asked him where he came from. He sighed, and said, 'From nowhere.' Then I asked him his name, and he sighed again, looked timidly around, and said, 'They used to call me Niels Bruus.' I shuddered, and said, 'That is a sinister name; someone of that name was murdered in these parts about twenty years ago.' He sighed even deeper, and muttered, 'It would have been better for me if I had died at the time; to flee the country has done me no good.' My hair stood on end, and I began to shake with horror, for now it seemed as if I could plainly recognize him again. Moreover, it was as if I were seeing the living image of Morten Bruus, whom I had buried three years previously. I backed away from him and crossed myself, thinking it was a ghost. But he sat down on the edge of the fireplace, and said, 'Alas, pastor, I hear that my brother Morten is dead. I went to Ingvorstrup, but the new owner drove me away. But tell me, is my old master, the Pastor of Vejlbye, still alive?' Suddenly the scales fell from my eyes, and I immediately grasped how the whole horrible story fitted together. But I was so dumbfounded that for some minutes I was quite unable to speak. 'Yes', he said, greedily eating the bread, 'it was Morten's fault, all of it – but did the parson come to any harm?' 'Niels, Niels', I cried, full of horror and loathing, 'you have a bloody crime on your conscience. On account of you the innocent man had to lose his life at the hands of the executioner.' Both bread and crutch slipped from the tramp's hands, and he himself almost fell into the fire. 'May God forgive you, Morten', he groaned, 'I don't mean that – I mean God forgive me my great sin. But you're only trying to scare me, aren't you? I have walked here right from far on the other side of Hamburg, and have never heard a word of this. But no one but you has recognized me, pastor, and I did not reveal myself to anyone else. And when I passed through Vejlbye and

asked whether the parson was still alive, they said he was.'
'That's the new one', I said, 'not the one you and your wicked brother did to death.' At this he began to wring his hands and to moan and groan, so I fully realized that he had been but a blind tool in the hands of the Devil; I even began to feel sincere pity for him. So I took him into my study, spoke some words of comfort, and succeeded in making him compose himself sufficiently to enable him to explain to me, in fits and starts, all the details of this hellish piece of villainy.

His brother Morten – an ungodly man – had conceived a deadly hatred of Pastor Søren of Vejlbye from the time that he refused him his daughter in marriage. So as soon as the pastor got rid of his former coachman he urged his brother to seek the place in his stead. 'And mark my words', he had said to Niels, 'when the opportunity arises we shall play a trick on that man in black, and that shall be no loss to you.' Niels, who was stubborn and coarse by nature, and also incited by Morten, soon started quarrelling with his master; and no sooner had he been struck for the first time than he made haste to tell his brother at Ingvorstrup.

'Just let him strike you once more', Morten had said, 'and he shall pay for it. Come and let me know immediately.'

It was then that he picked a quarrel with the pastor in the garden, and ran all the way to Ingvorstrup without stopping. The brothers met outside the farm, and Niels related what had happened. 'Did anyone see you on your way here?' asked Morten. Niels did not think so. 'In that case', said Morten, 'we'll give him a fright he'll not recover from the first two weeks.' Then Niels was led secretly into the farmhouse, where he remained hidden until evening. As soon as everyone had gone to bed they went together to a spot marking the boundary between three fields[4], where the body of a man of Niels's age, height and appearance had been buried two days previously (he had been working at Ingvorstrup, and had hanged himself there, as the rumour had it, from desperation over Bruus's tyranny and threats, though others said it was from unrequited love). They dug up the body, despite Niels's reluctance. But his brother made him – and they dragged the body home to the farm, for it was close by. Then Niels had to take off all his clothes, and they dressed the corpse in them again, piece by piece – even including an earring. This done, Morten gave the corpse a blow on the face with a spade, and one on the temple, and then stuffed the body in a sack until the following evening, when they carried it into the woods just outside Vejlbye.

Niels had asked his brother several times what he had a mind to do, and what all the preparations were for, but the latter had always replied, 'You don't need to bother about that – that's my business.' Out in the woods Morten said to him,

'Now go and fetch me one of the parson's everyday gowns, preferably the long green one I have seen him wear in the morning.' 'I don't dare to', Niels replied, 'for they are hanging in his bedroom.' 'Then I will', said his brother, 'and now you must be off, and never come here again. Here's a purse for you with a hundred rix-dollars. That should see you through until you can find work in southern parts – but far away, do you hear, where no one knows you. Call yourself by another name, and never set foot on Danish soil again. Walk at night and hide in the forest during the daytime. Here's a bag of food I have brought from the farmhouse; it should last you until you have crossed the border. Make haste, now, and don't ever return, if you hold your life dear.'

Niels did as he was bid, and at this the brothers parted – nor have they seen each other again since that very day. The fugitive had suffered many ills in foreign countries, had been recruited into the army, had served for many years, and had fought in the war, in which he became crippled. Poor, weak and wretched, he had resolved to visit his birthplace, and had made his way there despite much suffering and hardship.

Such, in brief, was that unfortunate man's story, the truth of which I was not, alas, in any doubt. And thus it became clear to me how my unhappy colleague had fallen victim to the most abject evil, to the delusion of the judge and the witnesses, and to his own credulous imagination. Alas, what kind of man is it that dares to set himself up as judge over his fellow men? Who dares say to his brother, 'Thou art deserving of death?' Vengeance is mine, I will repay, saith the Lord. Only He who gives life can take it. For the bitter martyrdom you have had to suffer here on earth may the Lord reward you in the hereafter with the boundless joy of eternal life!

I did not feel inclined to denounce this broken and repentant sinner, all the less because the judge was still alive, and it would have been cruel to inform him of his terrible mistake before he himself goes thither where all the hidden things of darkness will be brought to light. Thus I strove, instead, to offer him the solace of religion, and thereafter exhorted him in all seriousness to conceal from everyone his name and the entire story. On this condition I promised him refuge and care in the home of my brother, who lives far away from here.

The next day was a Sunday. When I returned home late in the evening from my other parish, the tramp had disappeared; but by the evening of the following day the story was known all over the neighbourhood. Driven by his uneasy conscience, he had rushed off to Rosmus and presented himself as the real Niels Bruus before Judge Sørensen and all his household. The judge suffered a stroke and died before the week was out, but on Tuesday morning Niels Bruus was found lying dead outside the door of Aalsøe Church on the grave of the late lamented Søren Qvist.

TARDY AWAKENING

I cannot recall any death that has caused greater sensation than that of my friend of many years, Dr L in R. People stopped one another on the street and rushed from one house to the other asking, 'Have you heard? Did you know? What could have been the reason? Could he have done it when delirious?' and so on. He was an extremely amiable man, universally liked and respected, an excellent doctor with a large practice; as it seemed, happily married; the father of six lovely children, of which the two eldest sons were already making their way in the world, the eldest daughter married to a worthy civil servant, the next eldest recently confirmed, and the two youngest ten and twelve years old. Furthermore, he was comfortably off, a hospitable host, and always the life and soul of the party. He had reached the age of forty-eight and never been ill.

Suddenly the rumour went that he was indisposed. His patients waited a whole day for him in vain. People enquired after him and came to visit him, but he would receive no one; the doctor was said either to be sleeping or not well enough to see anyone. The other doctor in the town was, if not exactly summoned, at least admitted. When people enquired about Dr L's condition he shrugged his shoulders, shook his head and declared that he did not know the cause of his illness. L would on no account take any medicine. And I, his pastor, was the only one he would receive daily for any length of time. He had no wish to see his children; if any of them entered the room he turned to face the wall. He lay like that for eight days, and on the ninth he shot himself. Since the other doctor declared that he had taken his life in a state of delirium he was given a Christian burial. I would have spoken some words over his grave, but my voice broke with grief, and I could scarcely utter the words of committal for tears.

Before his death I had learned from him the secret cause of this terrible step. But what had then been a secret could not remain so for long, because five people had shared it; and one of them, driven by jealousy and facile indignation, was unable to conceal the story of a crime that should rather have been buried with its unfortunate victim and brought only before the judgment seat of Our Lord the eternally righteous. What at that time was rumoured darkly by word of mouth can now be entrusted to paper, though with the omission of the names of those concerned. For of these, only three of Dr L's children, who in fact live abroad, and his widow – the chief protagonist in this tragedy – are still alive. But I shall begin my story a little further back. . . .

It was exactly twenty-five years prior to this grievous catastrophe that I, having graduated in theology, accepted the position as private tutor in R, where in those days the school had a bad reputation. I became acquainted with L shortly after my arrival, and not exactly in the most amicable fashion. He had recently settled in the town as a general practitioner, and we ran into one another at a ball. I was only one year older than he was – cheerful and lighthearted, and a skilful and impassioned dancer. I soon picked out the best dancer among the ladies; she was indisputably also the most beautiful, though I must confess that it was in the first capacity that she made the greatest impression on me. I asked her to be my partner in one of the dances then in current fashion, and she accepted with a bow. It was my turn to lead, and I had just clapped my hands as a signal to begin, when L – whom I had never seen before – stepped up to my partner and, bowing, reminded her that she had promised him that dance.

Miss W blushed, and made the excuse that she had thought it was the next dance she had agreed to dance with him. 'But if my partner permits', she added, 'we could still reverse the order.'

'By no means!' L replied, a trifle sarcastically, 'I shall withdraw, and resign myself to being No. 2, not least because

I am probably a poor dancer in comparison with this gentleman.'

'It makes no odds', I said, 'which of us is the best dancer. But if my partner's proposal does not please you, I beg you to let us begin – the entire quadrille is waiting for us.'

He was standing right between us. 'Both begin and end!' he retorted even more sarcastically, and stepped aside.

When I reached the end of the quadrille I saw him standing at the bottom with one of the clumsiest figures in the ballroom; and I noticed that he refused to give my partner his hand in the chain. She smiled almost imperceptibly at me, and I fancied I felt a soft pressure on my hand. The fellow was jealous, that was obvious. I imagined he must have had other rights than those decreed by the laws of the ballroom, so when the dance was over I went up to him and apologized for my curtness. This approach evoked a courteous response, and we were soon clinking our punch glasses in the hopes of a closer acquaintanceship.

Later I danced with Miss W again. As I took my leave of her, possibly kissing her hand with some warmth, I received and responded to the second pressure of her hand. I can assure you that this excited neither my heart nor my senses in the slightest; only my vanity was pleasantly tickled. I had on other occasions received such secret signs from a girl's fair hand in the heat and pleasurable whirl of the dance; but I realized that such manifestations – often involuntary – of the tender emotions of a happy heart are usually just as fleeting as the greetings exchanged by two wayfarers in passing, and promptly forgotten. But when, a couple of months later, I learned that Miss W had already been secretly betrothed to L at the time, I made a mental note of these pressures of the hand. A girl who is free and unpledged may venture such a thing – even though she ventures more than she may realize or suspect. But when an affianced girl permits herself such advances she gives the impression of being a coquette; and were she a married woman, she would be regarded by any not totally inexperienced dancing partner as what she either is or will become – a whore. However, that was the first and last time I noticed anything suspicious about Miss W, and as I have since been witness to her virtuous and moral character and conduct both as a young girl and a wife, I had begun to believe I had been mistaken about her and the significance of her action, for she may not even have been conscious of it.

To me it has been a strange and indeed often sad experience, confirmed on far too many occasions, to find that my first impression of a person's face, or rather, countenance, is to be relied upon, in that it provides a trustworthy glimpse into the heart – an accurate impression of the person's true character. I have often reproached myself for what I myself regarded as a fancy. Indeed I have often punished myself for my stern and unmotivated judgments and silently made amends for that secret offence when, subsequently, I have observed behaviour quite contrary to what my first impression had led me to suppose – and above all when I observed not only a totally different character but also quite a different face. And yet ... Alas, I must painfully confess that reason has sooner or later been put to shame by an instinctive hunch; it was not so much the pressure of Miss W's hand as my first glance at her face that whispered to me: this lovely girl is not for one man alone. The look in her eyes was neither sweetly languishing nor ardently inviting, neither tenderly indulgent nor profoundly searching; her smile was neither sweet nor roguish, and, still less, was it bold; the movements of her straight and perfectly proportioned figure had nothing voluptuous about them – nothing that betrayed sensual lust. And yet in this gentle, composed face there lay something enigmatic, something hidden; it seemed to conceal a deep, dreadful secret, or rather – to portend a crime, not yet conceived, that only the future would bring to light. After the lapse of twenty-five years I was reminded most cruelly of this long-forgotten premonition.

Should vampires be other than the abortive fancies of an unbridled imagination, then I have indeed seen one of these creatures – outwardly alive, inwardly lifeless, bodies without souls, flesh without a heart.

I have known her as an eighteen-year-old girl, and as a wife and mother. I have seen her among the dancers and among the

worshippers, with playing cards in her hands and with a babe at her breast, at her daughter's wedding and beside the dead body of her husband. But she was always the same – gentle, calm, attentive, and perfectly composed. I have seen her recently – she is now not far short of fifty – but she has hardly changed: she enjoys perfect health, and always displays the same unruffled cheerfulness. To me the darkest days of the year (after the sorrowful event that took place while I was living in R) were the two on which I had to give her the Holy sacrament. Sometimes I tried to arouse her conscience in my sermons, but there was nothing to arouse. If she should happen to see these pages I am sure she would be able to read them without dropping a stitch or making a single mistake in her sewing.

But I am anticipating the course of events too much, and must return to where I left off. . . .

My acquaintanceship with L, which had begun so badly, continued and soon ripened into a friendship that only death has been able to terminate. Three months after the ball in question he confessed that he was secretly betrothed to Miss W, and had already been so at the time. All at once I recalled the pressure of her hand, and asked him – though without revealing my suspicions – whether he had not only taken counsel with his heart but also with his reason, whether he really knew her, and whether he was sure that she both would and could make him happy. He replied with the tender outpourings of a loving heart, assuring me that she loved just as deeply and sincerely as he did but also that she had such perfect self-control that no one had ever suspected her inclination. This was all the more necessary, in that a strict and hardhearted father would undoubtedly have forbidden her connection with a young man without any fixed means of livelihood. As soon as he acquired such a position he would ask for her hand, and was quite convinced that her parents would give their consent.

Six months later the district doctor in R died; L became his successor and – shortly afterwards – Elise W's happy husband. I have never seen a happier man – he was almost beside himself with sheer joy. He could neither sit nor stand in one place for any length of time; love's sweet restlessness drove him hither and dither, and eventually – as soon as it was at all possible – back into the fairy's magic circle. During these honeymoon days – which became weeks and months – his patients received only brief visits and brief prescriptions, though on the other hand the most comforting and cheering prognoses. For throughout this period no illness was fatal – both illness and death were under his control. In truth – I can remember it very well – his cures were all successful. I almost think he cured his patients with his happy face and cheerful talk. His wife too seemed quite happy, though her joy was tinged with moderation. The wife was no different than the sweetheart, and the bridal bed had not brought about any visible change in her.

Once, when he described his state of bliss to me in exalted terms, I couldn't help expressing the hope that she felt equally as much for him.

'Wilhelm', he whispered, '... *Die holde Sittsamkeit bey Tage.*'[1] Here he stopped, laid one hand on his breast and put the fingertips of the other to his lips, gazing heavenwards in rapture.

'Excellent,' I said, smiling, and never asked for any further explanation. Nevertheless I have always doubted whether one would discover any appreciable emotion beneath that calm, unruffled exterior. If there were any warmth in that beautiful body, I felt that it would be what I might call – if that were not a contradiction in terms – a cold fire, or just a smouldering ember, which could never burst into flames and perhaps just as little be extinguished.

Eight months after the wedding Elise presented her radiant husband with his first-born son. The birth was celebrated with much ado, coinciding as it did with the season when Phoebus and Bacchus were inseparable guests at any gathering – when they were constantly exerting a considerable reciprocal effect on one another and an irresistible influence on all their worshippers. The cup had to be initiated with song, and the song be concluded with toasts. The final toast was to me: when the party drew to a close I was presented with the letter confirming my appointment as curate in R. Two years later the incumbent himself retired and I married my Henriette, to whom I had been betrothed ever since my first student days. We kept up regular and always extremely friendly contact with L and his family.

His wife had given birth to their second son and mine to her first-born, when a third family joined our circle. A certain Lieutenant H was transferred to the regiment garrisoned in R. He was one of the most amiable and cultured officers I have ever known, and married to a lady who was beautiful, intelligent and lightheartedness itself.

The doctor and the lieutenant (or captain, rather, for he rapidly advanced) lived next-door to one another, while I lived opposite the doctor. In view of this, among ourselves we called our little closed circle 'the triangle'. L was the right-angle, H was one of the acute angles and I was the other one. Every Wednesday evening we would gather in one of the angles, but apart from this L and H often gave bigger parties, which they called circles, for they were both comfortably off; the former had a handsome inheritance from his father-in-law, the latter, from his own parents.

We lived in a state that to me often seemed too happy to last. The only thing the captain lacked was children, but he had on the other hand an abundance of cheerfulness.

We three men had undeniably the three most beautiful and virtuous wives in R. Nevertheless their characters and temperaments were vastly different, and precisely this divergence was – I believe – the explanation of the perfect harmony between them. My wife was quiet, friendly and shy; she appeared to submit to the other two, although she really had the deepest feelings and was the most intelligent. Mrs H was always jolly, and full of fun and frolics, so she always led the conversation. Mrs L was quiet, but her entire way of being had something impressive about it – something that suggested a superior intellect, which she never, however, attempted to assert. So she was treated by the others like an elder sister, although she was both the youngest and the least educated.

If similarity in character were the condition for marital happiness we six people should have been differently matched – there should have been a complete change-about. My even temper, my natural sedateness, which, owing to the dignity of my office, took firmer and firmer hold of me, should really have been united with Mrs L. Her jovial, frank, lively and breezy husband would have found the most like-minded partner in Mrs H. And my gentle, meek and devout wife should have been chosen to accompany the captain on his path through life.

The only thing military about Captain H was in fact his uniform. In civilian clothes he looked as modest and shy as a new-baked student. Not that he wasn't a capable officer; he was renowned as such by the entire regiment – by his fellow officers and the ranks alike. On parade his company was always the smartest, even though his men were better acquainted with his purse than with his swagger cane, which merely dangled from his wrist for the sake of appearances. His courage, integrity and nobility of mind were recognized and appreciated by all. He was frequently chosen to mediate in the event of a dispute, and prevented in this capacity many a duel. In short: he was an extremely charming man, and far more of a danger to female hearts than he himself seemed to be aware of.

How we all longed for Wednesdays! We used to gather at teatime, whereupon we devoted a couple of hours to music, in which all of us – excepting Mrs L – took an active and by no means unsuccessful part. After supper we three gentlemen played a serious game of Hombre, while the ladies chatted in private, much enlivened by Mrs H's sallies and hearty laughter. On more than one occasion the latter brought about a penalty or hindered a perfect *codille*, driving us from our card-table over to our merry wives.

A year or so passed in this fashion without anything to disturb our mutual friendship and cheerfulness. But suddenly a noticeable change took place in the captain: he was often absent-minded, and made serious mistakes both in our music-making and in Hombre. Sometimes he was gloomy and taciturn, at other times ebullient and unusually talkative, though his talk was somewhat incoherent. My wife drew my attention to this strange transformation, hinting that she feared something was going on between him and Mrs L. I hushed her and endeavoured to reassure her in this respect. But, alas ... I knew more than she did. I had been a witness against my will to a scene that will never be erased from my memory, and which gave me enough to speculate about for a long while.

We had been talking for some time about giving a masked ball, and I believe Mrs L had been the first to bring up the idea. At last everything was arranged, the masks and costumes procured and the evening decided upon – it was to be held at the club. Since my cloth prohibited me from participating in such entertainments I had arranged a card party with three other of the town's Hombre-players. Towards evening I developed one of my customary headaches and got someone to take over my hand, intending to take a nap, as I usually did. So I asked my host to show me to a quiet and out-of-the-way room, hoping that half an hour's rest would banish my pain. I was shown a room far enough away from the ballroom that the faint sound of music and other noises only served to make me sleepy. I sat down to dose in an armchair, which was standing in a corner by the window.

I had not been asleep very long when I was awakened by the sound of the door creaking. Two people entered the room – that I could hear, though I couldn't see anyone because it was quite dark. It was obviously a man and a woman; but both were masked – I could tell that from their muffled voices.

'Well, and what is it you want, my dearest?' he said.

'Sweet husband', lisped a female voice, 'you look so attractive tonight.'

'But dear wife', he replied, 'what's the matter with you? Do we really need to meet in stealth, as if we were treading forbidden paths?'

No answer – the sound of a 'kiss' made me suspect that they had unmasked themselves. I sat as if on tenterhooks. What was I to do? My headache, now even worse as the result of this sudden awakening, rendered me unable to take any decision. The door creaked again; but whether they left the room or remained there I did not know. Everything was now quiet, and a brawl out in the yard was all that I heard. I sat like that for some time, listening in vain. I tried to fall asleep again; but the row in the yard became worse. Someone came out with a lantern or a candle, which cast its shadow through the window onto the sofa opposite. Invisible myself, there I saw Captain H in Mrs L's arms. Obviously a dreadful mistake had come about, but whether it was intentional on the one part or the other I could not then decide.

The captain jumped up with a cry of horror. Mrs L collapsed on the sofa, hiding her face in both her hands, as if in despair or shame. It became dark again.

'God forgive us both,' he said. 'Eternal silence, and – were it only possible – eternal oblivion.'

She seemed to me to be sobbing. He uttered a painful sigh, and went out; shortly afterwards she followed him, and I was left alone.

I remained there for some time, quite confused and stunned by what I had unwittingly seen. When I entered the ballroom again, the guests had just unmasked themselves. The doctor and the captain were identically attired – as Don Juan. Mrs H wore Turkish costume. Mrs L had definitely been wearing an identical costume when I saw her on the sofa; but now she was a shepherdess – this I found both remarkable and suspicious. The doctor was in excellent spirits: he was teasing Mrs H, insisting that she had encountered him alone in the passage and embraced him, thinking he was the captain. The latter, who was standing nearby, tried to laugh, but the attempt was unsuccessful and ended in a forced cough. Mrs L's face revealed not the slightest change; she was smiling just as serenely as she usually did at the playful remarks of all her friends. I began to distrust my own eyes; had she been guilty, how would she then have been able to preserve such – what I might call – infernal calm. Of course the Turkish woman in that room could have been someone else who resembled her; my headache could have deprived my senses of their acuteness, and so on. In short, I had almost regained my belief in her innocence, when some time afterwards my wife – an excellent observer – told me in confidence that she was afraid that the suspicion she had previously expressed was not totally unfounded. Indeed it was plain to see that the captain had undergone a profound change since the masked ball: he was often distracted and wrapped up in his own thoughts; he had lost his former cheerfulness and acquired in its stead a curious gaiety that broke through in fits and starts, often without reasonable cause. The reason for this change – his guilty conscience – was of course known to me, but I kept this from my wife. I tried to defend Mrs L, but did not launch into any explanation as regards the captain.

'My dear', I said, 'beware of casting suspicion on anyone – it is quite unlike you. Do you actually know something? Have you seen anything?'

'Just a single glance,' she replied. 'But it was a glance that made him blush and me turn pale – so we must both of us have understood it. It was as quick as a distant flash of lightning on a cloud in the night sky, but clear enough to illuminate it. The two of them were alone in the room, but I saw it reflected in the mirror.'

I shook my head as if I didn't believe her, and told her not to talk about it. 'We will not even discuss the matter among ourselves,' I said. 'You could so easily be mistaken in your conjectures. A glance can be interpreted in many ways – why do you assume the worst?'

She too shook her head, and the subject was not brought up again – for twenty whole years.

In the meantime my wife and I continued our secret and quite independent observations, but discovered nothing – not the slightest thing. The captain gradually regained, if not his former frank cheerfulness, then a certain bearing, which had a tinge of something more serious – possibly more subdued – about it. He was of course getting older for every day, and the sweet hopes of fatherhood were fast diminishing. Time, which rolls us along on our course, rubs all the sharp edges off our youthful emotions; imperceptibly we become either firm or flexible, strong or lethargic, until eventually all passions desert us in order to start their game with younger and softer hearts.

The triangle remained intact, the circles likewise. We had our musical evenings; we played our Hombre. Our children grew up, adding their voices to ours in the former and replacing us at the card-table when the newspaper reports distracted our attention.

The doctor's two eldest sons had taken their degrees in medicine and surgery, mine in theology. His eldest daughter was married and mine engaged, when the volcano that had for so long been secretly smouldering in the darkness broke through its crust of secrecy and – with its unexpected eruption – destroyed the worldly happiness of two families.

I had just got home from a journey lasting several days when my wife received me with the sad news that the major was very ill. I threw off my travelling clothes and hurried accross. He was asleep. With an anxious expression on her face, his wife stood at the head of the bed, clasping her hands; she greeted me with a pained smile. I approached quietly and asked in a whisper how her dear patient was. She just shook her head, as she continued to regard him through her welling tears. His sleep was troubled, his lips and fingers in constant movement and his eyes rolling incessantly under their lids.

I sat down to wait for him to wake up. Meanwhile his wife's aunt told me the reason and course of his illness. Three days ago he had caught a cold when drilling his men, had felt very hot and drunk some cold water, had felt unwell shortly after he arrived home and had gone to bed, had rapidly deteriorated and suffered feverish attacks every afternoon. Our friend, the doctor, who visited him several times a day, comforted him as always, but had nevertheless seemed somewhat worried. At that point Mrs H hinted that there was something she would like her aunt to do, and the latter left the room.

Shortly afterwards the major woke up. His gaze was flickering; one could tell immediately that he was not fully conscious. He glanced at his wife and threw himself back in the bed in terror.

'Elise . . .', he began (the major's wife was called Charlotte), 'Elise, what do you want from me? It must be enough now – you're going too far. If the doctor or my wife saw you here in bed with me, what would they say? Go away, and leave me alone!' He stretched out both hands in front of him as if to push someone away.

His wife's eyes met mine – she changed colour. The sick man went on rambling, 'It was an unfortunate idea, that Turkish costume – I had no reason to suppose that you were not my wife...' Mrs H was listening anxiously. I could clearly see that she couldn't make out what he was talking about, but I understood him only too well – I still had a vivid recollection of the scene at the masked ball.

I went over to the poor woman and seized her hand. 'Compose yourself, my dear,' I said. 'Your husband's illness should now be at its peak – he is delirious.'

She answered merely with a deep sigh.

'Hush, hush!' the major whispered. 'They might hear us down below – they know that the uniform depot is just above the mangling room, Elise, and think if anyone should discover the secret door in the summerhouse. . . .'

The major's wife clutched hold of the bedpost. She turned pale – a terrible change came over her face.

'Dear lady', I said, pretending only to notice one reason for her emotion, 'wouldn't it be best to send for the doctor? His presence might perhaps set our minds at rest – this crisis is probably not as dangerous as it appears.' She nodded in reply and hurried out.

The patient's eyes closed – he slept, but restlessly. I glanced out into the yard. Mrs H was walking rapidly over to the mangling room. The uniform depot was in fact directly above this, and the summerhouse in the doctor's garden – a two-storey wooden building – was immediately adjacent to it. I suddenly had a horrible suspicion, which was close to becoming a certainty. During the summer I had often had tea or played Hombre in that very summerhouse, and could remember that from there it was very easy to hear if there was someone in the depot. The patient's fantasies must undoubtedly be founded on the lamentable truth.

While Mrs H was outside – most likely in order to investigate whether there was any truth in what had just been hinted at – the doctor came of his own accord. With a troubled expression he went over to the bed, looked at the sick man, felt his pulse, looked anxiously at me, and shook his head.

The major woke up – he stared fixedly and horror-struck at the doctor. 'What?' he exclaimed. 'What does this mean? You gave me to believe that your husband had gone to visit a patient in the country and would be away for the night, and here he is, standing as large as life in front of me. Why did you set out to fool me? Why did you give the signal we agreed upon? Didn't you pin the red ribbon onto the curtain in the summerhouse? Go away, and sleep with your own husband! You are becoming far too rash, and the pitcher may go to the well once too often.'

I was standing as if on hot coals. I drew the doctor over to the window, wishing to prevent him from hearing or remarking anything further.

'What do you think?' I asked.

'He is delirious,' he replied. 'The illness is taking a bad turn.'

'His ideas are quite wild,' I pursued.

'Oh, no!' shouted the major, who had heard what I said. 'I know quite well what I'm saying, and I shall tell you once and for all, Mrs L – there shall be nothing further between us. It's a sin against both your husband and my wife, and neither of them deserves that from us.'

At this the doctor pricked up his ears. He cast a quick glance at the summerhouse; the upper window could be seen from the sickroom. I followed the direction of his gaze, and – inside the window – the major's wife was standing with raised, clenched hands; but in the next moment she had disappeared. Good God! She must, then, have discovered the secret passage that the feverish patient was raving about. The latter had fallen asleep again.

The doctor turned pale. I took his hand and whispered, 'For God's sake, dear friend, surely you never take what anyone says in a delirium seriously? In a paroxysm of fever like that a patient can imagine the most preposterous things.' He looked thoughtfully at me, but did not answer. His glance conveyed something interpretable as, 'You don't mean what you're saying.' In the same moment the major's wife entered. Her face was flushed – she looked almost as excited as the sick man. The doctor went calmly up to her, comforted her, and asked a few questions with regard to the patient. She answered them briefly and carelessly, her glance fluttering restlessly from the one to the other. But soon her anxiety dissolved in a flood of tears; she rushed over to the bed, dropped down onto her knees and pressed the sick man's hand to her bosom.

'Oh God', she prayed hastily in a low voice, 'spare his life just this once, so that he can receive my forgiveness if he is guilty, or my remorse if I am doing him an injustice.' (I only heard half of what she said, but was able to fill in the rest. The doctor heard none of it, however, for he hadn't been listening.) 'You unhappy man', she continued, pressing her forehead against his hand, 'it is you who have been seduced, while she ...' At this she jumped up and turned to the doctor.

I caught hold of her hand and pressed it hard. 'Right now', I said, 'it is up to the doctor alone to speak. Control your fear and your anguish ...' And in an undertone so that he shouldn't hear, I added, '... if you value your husband's life.'

She composed herself and suppressed the pernicious words that were already hovering on her lips. She had one of those happy dispositions that combine great passion with a quick judgment and lively intelligence that the former is never quite able to obscure. Her heart was tender but by no means weak. Alas, it did not, however, prove strong enough to stand up to the far more dangerous test to which it was to be subjected.

A message arrived – I had to go and attend to my official duties. Mrs H followed me outside, and there I did everything I could to reassure her as regards her husband's wild innuendos.

'Since I too', I admonished her, 'have been a witness to these, you cannot regard it as presumptuous meddling in your marital affairs if I mention them. I am able to view more calmly and with greater detachment what may easily blind and bewilder a loving eye. Probability is not always synonymous with the truth, and there may be many other possible interpretations apart from the worst one. Do, for heaven's sake, bring your usually so sound judgment to bear, and spare yourself and your sick husband. And don't whatever you do let the doctor get the slightest inkling of this, or the situation may prove doubly unfortunate, and yet nevertheless rest on a mistake.'

Sighing, she pressed my hand and returned to the sickroom.

I had a lot of things to do; my work had piled up in my

absence. This had been in the morning, and it was not until towards evening that I was free. I wanted to go and see the major again, but decided first to speak to the doctor in his own home in order to learn what he really thought about our friend's illness.

His wife was out in the country with their second-eldest grown-up daughter; the two youngest had been invited out here in the town. The maid told me that the doctor was in his study. I went up.

He stood facing the door with his back to his bureau. He was clutching some papers in his left hand, while pressing his right hand convulsively against his breast. His face reflected that cold, mute despair that admits neither hope nor fear. My heart froze; I immediately saw that everything must have been discovered, and that suspicion had ripened into certainty. He glanced at me casually, as if he didn't know me.

How would comfort be able to penetrate a heart that had been coated with ice by the wintry storms of misfortune? I lifted my hands in prayer to the Lord, whose mercy begins where hope ends.

I know nothing more difficult – no more dubious task than that of comforting those who have most need of comfort: that is to say, those who cannot comfort themselves. To say to someone whose entire worldly happiness has been destroyed in one go, 'Be a man! Fight! *tu contra audentius ito* . . .$^{2\prime}$ is the same as saying to someone who has fallen and broken his leg, 'Come over to me and I'll help you up', or to someone unable to swim who has fallen into a raging current, 'Exert yourself! You can easily save your skin if you really want to.'

Some comfort the unhappy person with the hope he has lost; others with time, whose painfulness he or she is incapable of bearing; and still others – who would have done better to suffice with their silent sympathy and compassionate weeping – act as Job's comforters, in that they hint at God's punishment, at sins deliberately and secretly committed: instead of pouring balsam on the wound, they drip venom into it. Indeed the sufferer may well answer them in the bitterness of his lacerated heart, 'I have heard many such things: miserable comforters are ye all. Shall vain words have an end? or what emboldeneth thee that thou answerest? I also could speak as ye do: if your soul were in my soul's stead, I could heap up words against you, and shake mine head at you.'

When anguish constricts the breast, when it cannot even give vent through the lips, what other than the silent tears of a compassionate friend could melt that frozen heart? Mine flowed profusely and wetted his hand, which I had drawn from his own breast to mine. Then in this unhappy man as well the floodgates were opened through which both grief and joy are emptied: he rested his brow against my breast and wept like a child.

But not for long. He threw back his head again, and the tears returned to their secret caverns. 'There, you see!' he cried, excitedly pressing the papers into my hand. 'These are prescriptions, legibly written – easy to understand – specific remedies for romantic whims, love – for faith in womanly virtue, in friendship....' He threw himself onto a chair, gnashing his teeth and emitting something that resembled laughter.

As I read the papers – letters whose contents I shall soon disclose – he stared fixedly at me with what I might almost call a look of envy, and with the kind of ghastly, bittersweet smile that is often seen long afterwards on the faces of those who have frozen to death.

The letter lying on top – which like the other two was presumably addressed to the major, but had neither date nor signature other than 'Your .. i ..' (Elise) – was undoubtedly the most recent, and read as follows:

'Yes, my beloved, I cannot, will not, conceal from you that beneath my far too weak heart I bear a secret pledge of our secret love. My conscience reproaches me for betraying my husband. But love knows of only one sin – infidelity towards the beloved. It has only one duty – to do everything for the cherished object of one's affection, to devote to it both body and soul, and even, if necessary, to sacrifice both. Frans, you were childless; it hurt me to the core. If I have forfeited my happiness in the hereafter, I have done it only to please you here on earth. Now, beloved, I have nothing more to give you.'

The second letter seems to have been written immediately after that unfortunate masked ball.

'What's done is done', she writes, 'but it is fate, mysterious fate itself, that has brought us together against our will and our better knowledge. Fate itself has united us – who shall then tear us apart? I feel it, I know it – since that night I am yours for ever, I have a new heart, a new soul. I am totally transformed; my thoughts, my desires have only one goal – you, beloved man that I adore! Oh, do not hate me, do not despise me! It is not sensuality that draws me to you – no, my love shall be pure. But I must speak to you – I must pour out the agonies of my heart, must beg forgiveness for a crime for which fate alone must stand responsible. I don't know what I am writing – at eleven o'clock tonight I shall expect you – my husband is in the country – have mercy on

your unhappy . . i . .'

'Secrecy . . .', said the third letter, which, chronologically, was most probably the middle one, 'is the life-principle of love; without this the myrtle lacks both root and stem. Though should anyone know that I loved you, that you were my wedded husband, I believe even the impossible would come true. But what a temple for our secret joys – a storeroom full of soldiers' uniforms and hempen cloth!

'This evening my husband is going to P. By eleven o'clock everyone will be in bed except she who awaits you with a burning heart. The sun does not rise until seven. Oh, it will be a long time before I say, "*Frantz! Frantz! Steh auf! der Morgen graut.*" '[3]

As soon as I had finished reading, and the last letter slipped from my trembling hand, L got up, took hold of my shoulders and asked with a piercing look, 'Well, my good pastor?'

'How', I said, 'have these letters come into your possession? Are you sure they are genuine?'

'As genuine', he cried, 'as *cortex peruviana selecta*[4], though not quite as beneficial to the health – and I have them straight from the paramour himself.'

(The unfortunate Mrs H told me later how it had happened. In the afternoon, when the doctor had come to see his patient again, the latter began once more to rave, and even more intelligibly than before. He had finally ordered her – whom he still took to be the doctor's wife – to bring him a certain drawer from the bureau. The drawer had a double bottom; on pressing a knob the uppermost one sprang up and the letters came to view. He had handed her these with the words: 'There, Elise, are your letters. Tear them up, or burn them!' She had torn up some other papers instead, and had gone behind his bed and read the *billet-doux*. No longer able to restrain herself, she had handed them to the doctor, and now the lot had fallen on the cruelly deceived man.)

'My poor, pitiable friend!' I sighed. 'What will you decide now? What will you do?' He let go of me, and walked up and down the room with rapid steps and clenched hands. 'What will I do?' he repeated several times.

'In the first place', I added, 'I suppose these fatal letters ought to be destroyed....'

'Destroyed!' he cried. 'These letters?' – he snatched them up again – 'What? These sweet, blessed pledges of love?' He pressed them to his breast with the vehemence of a lover. 'No, pastor, I cannot part with them. They shall follow me into the grave – and from the grave, up there where all such pledges shall one day be redeemed.'

'Oh, my friend, my friend!' I said. 'Surely they have already been registered there a long time ago? Why do you wish to be her accuser? Neither vengeance nor judgment belongs to you, but to a God, whose justice is far above our fleeting passions.'

He paused for a while, gazed heavenwards, and then gave them back to me. 'There', he said quietly. 'Keep them, destroy them! But promise me first, that when I am dead and gone you will show them to her.'

I promised, though added, 'Why, dear doctor, do you speak of death? You have had a hard, terrible blow. You are losing a wife whom you love – an unworthy, contemptible creature. But do you not still have your children?'

Staring fixedly at me, he burst into savage laughter. 'Whose children? My children? No – the major's children...'

'The two eldest', I interrupted, 'were born before he came to the town, and nobody, with the merest glance, can mistake their father.'

'And the others?' he asked, smiling bitterly. 'Which of them? How many of them are mine? Haven't you read the letter? Don't you think that they look the very image of him? O-oh', he said, striking his brow with his clenched fist, and started to pace the room again.

I was silent – I didn't know what to say in a hurry. Because when I thought it over, I felt that he could in fact be right, especially as regards the married daughter. Her likeness to the major was unmistakable. 'The imagination . . .', I murmured at last, rather slowly and half in doubt, 'may also affect. . . .'

'Aha!' he broke in. 'We don't need the help of the imagination here – the whore herself has confessed.'

At that moment the two youngest daughters entered the room, and ran over to embrace him. But he stepped as far back as he was able, raised his hands as if to push them away, while staring at them with an expression of horror and disgust. The poor little girls were terrified. Trembling, they burst into tears and flung their arms around one another – they were afraid they had done something wrong. I put my arms around them and my tears fell on their golden locks. Then his callousness turned to pity; his accustomed tenderness returned and – for a while – drove out the demon of doubt. He sat down, took them on his knee and caressed them in turn – the children now weeping with joy.

In this more favourable mood I felt I could safely leave him in order to attend to my unfinished tasks. I left him to the gentler feelings of his good heart and to the grace of our merciful and all-powerful Lord.

When I visited them the following morning he was lying in bed, undressed though awake. His twelve-year-old daughter – the next youngest – was sitting beside him, urging him to drink a cup of tea. He refused it, regarding us both with a cold, dark and almost distant expression. I pointed pleadingly at the child, and he took the cup, put it to his lips and tasted it; but as if it had been bitter medicine, he rested it on the counterpane again. In order to send the little girl out of the room I asked her to bring some lunch, and then attempted once more with kindly persuasion to open the poor man's sealed heart.

He put down the cup and folded his hands. Either he hadn't heard me or he didn't understand me. 'My life', he said at last, slowly and softly, 'is now forfeit to Him who gave it. The poison is working – I have emptied the cup to the very last drop, and for me there is no other antidote than death. I have awoken from a long sweet dream. As so often happens to the demented, I have had a lucid moment – a sure premonition of pending dissolution. Oh, my God, my God! Please take me away from here before that serpent returns!' He closed his eyes as if he feared the sight of her. 'I loved her so tenderly, so faithfully', he continued after a pause, 'with my whole heart and soul. For twenty years I imagined I was living in an earthly paradise, but I was walking on a volcano that was secretly smouldering under my feet. The thin crust that separated heaven and hell is now broken, and I have fallen into the flaming chasm. Oh, merciful God, let my body be consumed, and receive my poor soul!'

I prayed with him – prayed to Him for strength and patience. I comforted him with God's almighty goodness, with the thought of his two hopeful young sons, and of a more bearable future separated from his unworthy wife. He quietly shook his head. 'I cannot live', he said, 'in a world where she draws breath. We could no longer share a common sun. Separation from board and bed and house and native land – all that means nothing. There must be light and darkness, life and death, time and eternity between us – not until then are we separated.'

The eldest daughter (alas, I dare not call her *his* daughter) entered with her two-year-old child in her arms. The infant stretched out its arms towards its supposed grandfather, babbling the appellation that was previously so sweet to him. As if fraught by excruciating inner pain he turned his head away. The distressed mother put down the child, the tears streaming from her eyes. I had to lead them both away and to exert all my discretion and inventiveness in order to reassure the poor young woman. I was only partially successful – she had a presentiment of coming disaster.

As far as my time permitted it I remained with my unhappy friend, and was his guardian, attendant and comforter in the following seven days. I had a difficult task; I had both to care for him, to turn away visitors, and to reassure the children.

The other doctor called a couple of times unbidden, but as there was nothing he could do he eventually stayed away.

I wrote to the sons in Copenhagen, hoping that their presence might have a beneficial effect on the poor sufferer (they arrived only in time to accompany his dead body to the resting-place he had pined for and into which he had forcibly gained entry).

My friend became quieter, and more gloomy and taciturn for every day; he seemed to me to be hatching some terrible plan.

On the eighth day after the tragic discovery the major passed away; he had been lying in a kind of coma ever since, and died without having regained consciousness. I brought L the news; he received it with indifference, merely saying, 'We shall soon meet again.'

Mrs L was expected home the following day. I asked her husband what measures should be taken as regards her arrival, and if it wasn't better to send her away. But he replied that he was fully prepared for her arrival and that everything would fall into place. I had my misgivings, and told him so. With a calm smile, he gave me his hand, saying, 'If I then had a clear premonition of my death, would you grudge me the fulfilment of the only wish still remaining to my broken heart? Those chains that bound me to life are loosening link by link; there is only one left – as soon as I see her, it will break.'

These words could be interpreted in two different ways. I ought not simply to have assumed the worst; and yet I continued to dwell on this, bringing all the arguments of reason and religion to bear. Alas, reason is powerless where a despairing heart is concerned, and religion can only comfort those who have previously been guided by it. And Dr L had either been too frivolous or too happy to nourish any deep religious conviction. He may well have been a believer, but his faith was a brittle one that had never been tried and strengthened by any appreciable grief or hardship. He was a child of joy, and parted from his constant companion in life he became an easy prey to grief – to that most terrible of all the passions against which the weak human soul has to contend.

I stayed with him until far into the night. As I was about to leave he stretched out his arms to me and pressed a farewell kiss on my lips. A few tears still glistened in his dull eyes, and with an almost broken voice he said simply, 'Thank you – good-bye until we meet again!'

I went home and lay down half-undressed, resolved to return to him early the next morning, not only in order to keep watch over him, but also to prevent, if possible, the meeting between him and his faithless wife – or at least to be a probably highly necessary third party to the scene.

But, exhausted as I was, I overslept, and none of my family wished to disturb me. I was awaked with the ghastly news that Dr L had shot himself. I rushed over there; he was still lying in the bloody bed, pierced through the heart. None of his family was in there, but only the other doctor, the mayor and the housemaid. The latter had been present when it happened. She stated that with the doctor's permission she had watched over him in my stead; that his wife, who had been informed of her husband's illness by the eldest daughter, had hastily returned to town and entered the room at daybreak, unexpectedly. As soon as he saw her he had sat up in bed, spoken a few words in a language the maid had not understood, thereupon drawn out a pistol from under the coverlet and shot himself through the heart.

I shall not dwell on the misery that followed. At the beginning of this story I briefly indicated how the crime of a voluptuous and unscrupulous woman brought ruin upon two families; and to many others an anguish that lingered for a long time and will never wholly be forgotten.

THREE FESTIVAL EVES

A JUTLAND ROBBER STORY

EASTER EVE

If you, dear reader, have ever been to Snab Hill, where the assizes used to be held in olden days, a little towards the south you would have been able to see a tiny straggling village by the name of Wannet. Here none other than peasants live, or have probably ever lived.

And here, a couple of hundred years ago, there once lived a man called Ib. What his wife's name was, I have never been able to discover. But this much I do know: he had an only daughter called Maren, commonly known as Ma-Ib's. She is said to have been neat and comely, this young woman, and wherever she went the young men stole a glance at her out of the corner of their eyes. But she had no eyes for anyone but Sejer; he was also an only child, and his father too lived in Wannet.

As I was about to tell you, one day, on Easter Saturday, a man called in at Ib's place. He was dressed like a peasant, and was for that matter well-built, handsome and spirited, looking as if he could be around thirty. No one at Ib's place knew him, but he himself said he was a woodlander from the Lou area – that he had recently obtained the lease of his father's farm and was now on his way north to trade in charcoal. He had silver buttons on his coat and waistcoat, so it was plain to see that he was no beggar. They gave him both food and drink, while in the meantime he chatted about this and that. Then, smirking slightly, he turns to Ib and says, 'My mother's getting old, and I think I'll soon need a helpmate. Do you by any chance know of a capable woman? Money's no problem, for we can always settle on that, but she must have a pair of nimble hands – and not be too old either.'

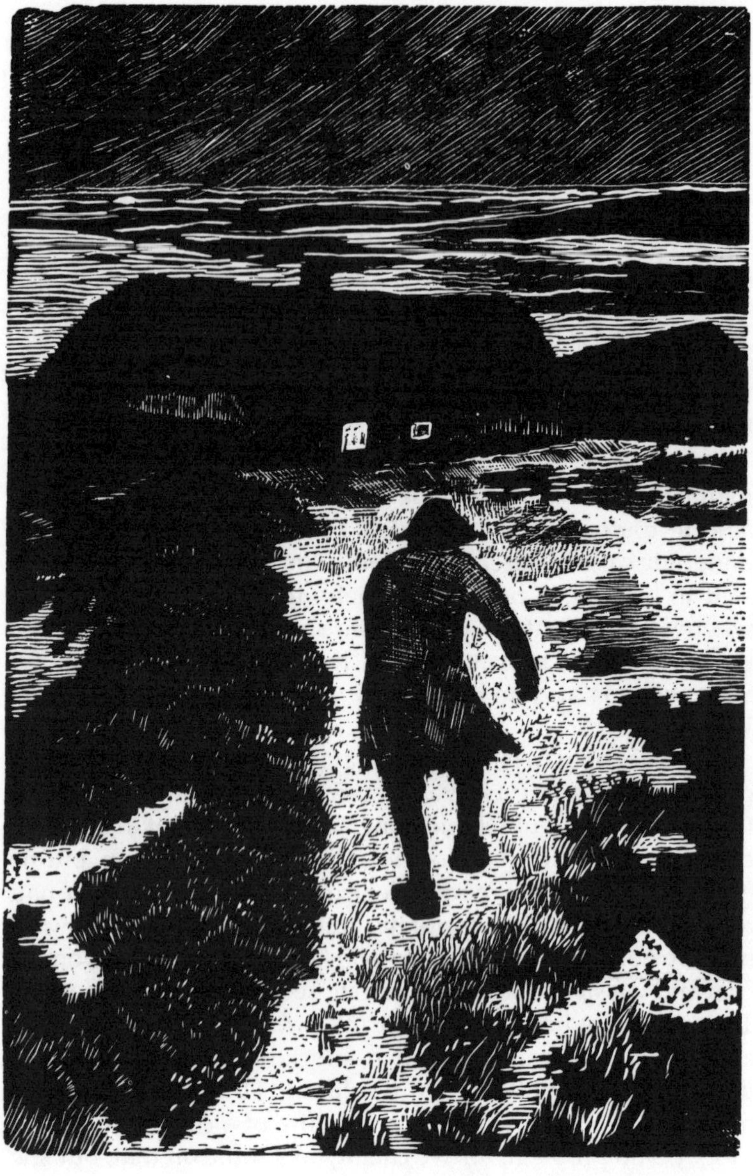

Ib appeared to show little interest. He scratched himself behind one ear, and said, 'H'm, a woman like that doesn't grow out of the heather-tufts every day' – and, glancing at his daughter, he laughed quietly. But his daughter didn't care for that talk and found some pretext to go out.

As the fellow was about to leave, Ib asked him his name. 'Well', he replied, 'my father was called Ole Breadless, so I suppose that must be my name too.' With that he left, but when he has got some way from the farm he meets Ma-Ib's, who has been over at Sejer's, and says to her: 'It can't help to beat about the bush, I have come for your sake alone. I'll come again at Whitsuntide, and you can think it over in the meantime. Now I bid you farewell!'

Ma-Ib's was not happy about that suitor. When she came home she sat down at the bottom end of the table, folded her hands in her lap and sighed deeply.

'What's that supposed to mean?' asked her father.

'I don't like that woodlander, or whatever he is', she answered. 'Aren't Sejer and I ever going to be able to get married?'

'On what?' retorted the old man. And no more was said. Both father and daughter got busy with their wool-winding.

Shortly afterwards Sejer enters. 'Good evening,' he says.

'Thank you,' they say.

'I'm going up to the manor', he says, 'to talk to the master, for it can't help bickering about it any longer.'

'A lot of good that'll do,' says Ib. 'The master's angry with you, and he'll pack you off to the army.'

'That may well be', says Sejer, 'but now we'll put it to the test.' And off he goes.

When he gets to Aunsbjerg and enters the gate he meets the lord of the manor himself, otherwise known as Jørgen Marswine.

'Are you coming here about your lease yet again?' he asks. 'It's no use – I've told you often enough.'

'Please, master', says Sejer, 'I must humbly implore you.'

Then his master looked at him angrily, lowered his brows and frowned, and it was plain for anyone to see that he

intended to fly at him and beat him there and then. But then he changed his mind, and his expression softened a bit. 'Listen,' he said. 'You know about these robbers who have been plundering and murdering people for so long, and are said to have their cave somewhere out on the moors. If you can find them and tie them up for me, then you won't have to pay a penny for your lease, and you shall have Ma-Ib's, and I shall even let you take a cart and two horses here from Aunsbjerg. Now you know how you stand.'

'God have mercy on me,' said Sejer, slinking away quite crestfallen. He ate nothing that evening, and Ma-Ib's didn't feel too good either. It was a wretched festival eve for them both.

WHITSUN EVE

From Easter to Whitsun time passed as well it might, and for the two young people everything was much as it had always been. They were not totally disconsolate, for they put their trust in the future – or in Him who is master of it.

On Whit Saturday Sejer went over to Ib's place – as he often did, I fancy – in order to hear if she might accompany him to Aunsbjerg Woods the following afternoon when they came home from Sørslev Church. It was an old custom in those parts – and still is, I believe – that on the first day of the holiday they gathered there in the open to dance. The Saturday in question, when Sejer went to visit his sweetheart, she was already dressed in her Sunday best.

'Good-day,' Maren, he says. 'What's going on? Why are you looking so fine today?'

'I came to think', she says, 'that I ought to go and see her ladyship and ask her to put in a good word for us with the master.'

'H'm', he says, 'that might bring us luck. I'll come too, and wait outside while you're inside with her.' So off they went.

As she walked up to the manor he sat down on a stone beside the entrance. And just then a cart came rumbling on its way to the saw-pit with a huge oak log. But the horses were small and emaciated, and in the middle of the gateway they could no more. The man – it was a villein who had been given this job – kept whipping the nags, but they couldn't shift the cart. Then the forester came up and told him off, and then the bailiff, and finally the honourable and well-born Jørgen Marswine. And they all scolded the peasant for meeting up with such jades – I can imagine they were the best he had.

Sejer sits watching all this; and now and again he smirks at all the fuss they are making.

The master notices this, and says, 'What are you sitting there grinning for?'

'I was thinking', he says, 'that the load is no heavier than that I could pull it alone.'

'Hey there! Unharness the horses!' his lordship shouts at the driver. And when that was done he says to Sejer, 'Get to work, then, and if you can pull the cart I'll give you what's on it. But if you can't, you shall up and have a ride on the wooden horse[1].'

Then the lad began to make excuses and said that he was only joking. But the master said that he would teach him to joke in his presence, and it was to be either one thing or the other.

'Well', said Sejer, 'if I have to, I have to,' whereupon he went up to the cart, removed the pole and got hold of the traces, bent over forwards and heaved – and after him followed the cart. But he trod so heavily on the ground that his wooden shoes went to pieces.

'You're no weakling.' said his lordship. And he was no weakling himself either, for people still relate that when he rode out of the gate he could grab hold of an iron ring on the lintel and raise his horse off the ground with his legs. 'Take the log, then, and find out for yourself how to get it home. And as far as the lease is concerned we'll see how things go.'

If anyone was happy, it was Sejer! And he thanked his

master, toppled the log onto the ground and sat down on it, looking out for his Maren through the gate. It was ages before she finally came, looking extremely woebegone. 'God have mercy on us wretched people!' she says – it was all she could do not to cry. 'We can never have one another.'

'That's some bad news you've brought,' says Sejer. 'The master half promised me that out here – what's come over him now?'

'So did the mistress,' she says. 'But now you shall hear what bad luck I had. When I've got upstairs and into the narrow passage, a fine gentleman comes towards me and seems to be looking at me – I couldn't get past him because he stood in my way – and he says, "You're..." (how he could swear!) "... the loveliest maid or mistress, or whatever you are, I've seen in this country. Listen, will you be good to me?"

'"No", I say, "I may not."

'"If you wish", he says, "then you may. I am Baron..." – I can't remember now what it was he called himself – "Just come here this evening, and my servant will keep a look-out and show you up to me."

'"No", I say, "it's sinful. Besides, I have a sweetheart and I mustn't deceive him." Then he held out a handful of money, but I slipped past him and into the mistress. She was very gracious towards me, and the master came in too and it sounded as if he would grant my request. But then this Baron fellow came in and listened to what we were saying, and he says, "If it's a decent fellow she wants, then he ought not to take her, for she's a shameless hussy – I saw how she stood flirting with one of the servants out in the passage." After the brute had lied about me like that, his lordship and her ladyship told me off and ordered me to be gone and never to show my face again.'

'Good gracious, Maren', said Sejer, 'is that all you get for your virtue and for being true to poor me? But – Our Lord is still with us, we must not give up hope. Something tells me that we shall have each other yet – though there be as many lords and ladies as there are leaves in Aunsbjerg Woods.'

Ma-Ib's sighed as if her heart were fit to burst, but said nothing. He said very little else until they reached Wannet and were to part company. Then she says, 'Good-night, Sejer, and thank you!'

'Thank you too, Maren,' he says. 'You have suffered enough for my sake; I'm afraid I can never make it up to you – only God can!'

'Do you want to go dancing in the woods tomorrow?' the girl asked him.

'Do you?' he asked in return.

'No,' she said. 'I don't feel like it.'

'Neither do I,' he said.

'Then I bid you good-night,' she said, giving him her hand.

'The same to you,' he replied, and at this they parted.

But there was more trouble in store for poor Maren, before she could get to bed. When she went in, *he* was sitting there – Ole Breadless, the woodlander. 'Is that you, sweetheart?' he says. 'Have you thought it over?'

'What?' she asks.

'Have you forgotten?' he says. 'It's no longer ago than Easter – it was about coming to live with me. Look here! So that you shouldn't think I go courting on thin ale and dry bread, I'll give you this as a betrothal gift.' He held out a heavy silver necklace with a heart-shaped pendant of the same metal. 'If you'd known the woman who wore it while she was alive, you'd never have accused her of being a barefoot peasant-girl!' And with these words he gave the father such a strange look that the daughter was seized with secret anxiety. The old man started, not knowing whether to believe his own eyes; none of them said a word.

'Well, do you want it?' Ole repeated.

'No,' stammered the girl, on her way out to seek comfort from her sweetheart. But the terrible suitor seized her arm with one hand, and, stowing the trinket away with the other, he said: 'The third time I come, I'll not take no for an answer.' And without any further farewells he took his hat and stick and walked off.

'The boy is coming with the cows now', said Ib, sitting down on the milking stool. Ma-Ib's went out to milk, but she didn't sing as she usually did at her work. Sejer watered his father's horses, but he didn't whistle as usual. It was a wretched festival eve for them both.

CHRISTMAS EVE

It was at dusk when an old tramp came shambling wearily over to Wannet to beg for a morsel of food in the name of God. He also called in at Ib's. They told him to sit down beside the kitchen door, and he would get a bite to eat and something for his bag.

When he had eaten he complained that it was too late and too cold to get any farther that evening, and begged Ib's folk for a night's shelter. To this they agreed, and showed him the inside of the oven, which was still warm from baking. The old codger crawled inside and lay down.

Night was falling. They had eaten their sweet porridge and whatever they had to follow, they had given the animals their evening fodder and bolted the door; they had sung their customary Christmas hymn, and started to get ready for bed. But now you shall hear what the old codger got up to: he crept out of the oven, unbolted the door and released the hook. And no sooner had he done so when five stalwart men appeared and entered the room, the tramp with them. But now he could tread on the floor just as briskly as they could. You see, they were the very robbers that his lordship at Aunsbjerg wanted Sejer to find and tie up, and the tramp was the father of the other five.

Things didn't look too good for poor Ib and his folk. He and his old mother and his daughter thought their last hour had come, and were so terrified that it was all they could do to beg for mercy.

The biggest and oldest of the young robbers – and that was none other than the woodlander – did the talking, and said, 'First bring us what the house can provide, and we can talk about the rest later.'

Ma-Ib's reached for the door latch. But the robber said, 'You just stay here, and let that old crone bring it in. For you might very well take it into your head to run loose, and we should like to have a bit of fun and games with you when we have eaten and drunk our fill.'

The girl collapsed into a chair, almost fainting from sheer fright. Ib sat on the edge of the bed, clasped his hands and prayed to Our Lord, who has the power to save whom He will. The old woman put everything they had of food and drink on the table, and it was remarkable to see how she managed.

But now you shall hear what happened next. Ib had a cowherd – a mere lad. He has lain down to sleep in a bench behind the stove and overhears all that is said. So he stealthily pulls on his stockings and breeches and creeps out with the old woman when she goes out into the kitchen to relight the candle one of the robbers has accidentally extinguished. Then he runs over to the neighbouring farm to tell Sejer how things are at their place.

It took Sejer no time to think up a plan. 'Take that mouse-eared horse of ours', he said, 'ride as fast as you can to Aunsbjerg and tell them what's going on, and say that if they hurry down here they may be able to catch all the robbers before they make off again!'

The boy rushed out, leapt onto the horse and rode away.

Sejer grabbled hold of a wooden flail and hurried over to Ib's place. There he found all six scoundrels sitting on one of the long benches with their backs to the windows. 'What kind of a fellow are you?' they shouted at him. 'You must want your belly ripped open!' At this they got up, intending to seize him. But he was too quick for them; he got hold of the oak table and tipped it over on top of them, squeezing them against the wall with the edge of the table. 'Now I shall see if I can squeeze *your* bellies,' he said, and, pinning them down with one hand, he swung the flail and threatened to break any arm that moved. The eldest one tried to push the table over again nevertheless, but he instantly got such a blow on the arm that it hung down limp beside him. After that they all sat as quiet as mice and merely begged Sejer not to squeeze so hard.

Ib too had plucked up courage and, seizing a big axe, he

took his place on one side of Sejer, with Ma-Ib's on the other side with the poker. That was how things were, and it was not at all pleasant for either party. The robbers were in agony, dreading how this tight squeeze might end; and they couldn't make out what Sejer had in mind or how soon it would be put into effect – that made the pain even worse. Ib and his daughter were in the same agony of suspense, because Sejer couldn't very well blurt out what or for whom he was waiting. And for him, you may be sure, it seemed a long wait; for if the folk from the manor delayed too long or never showed up at all – the lad could have fallen off the horse on the way – what then?

At last his lordship arrived from Aunsbjerg with seven or eight men, and he was by no means the last to enter when the door flew open. But there they stood: how quiet it was in the

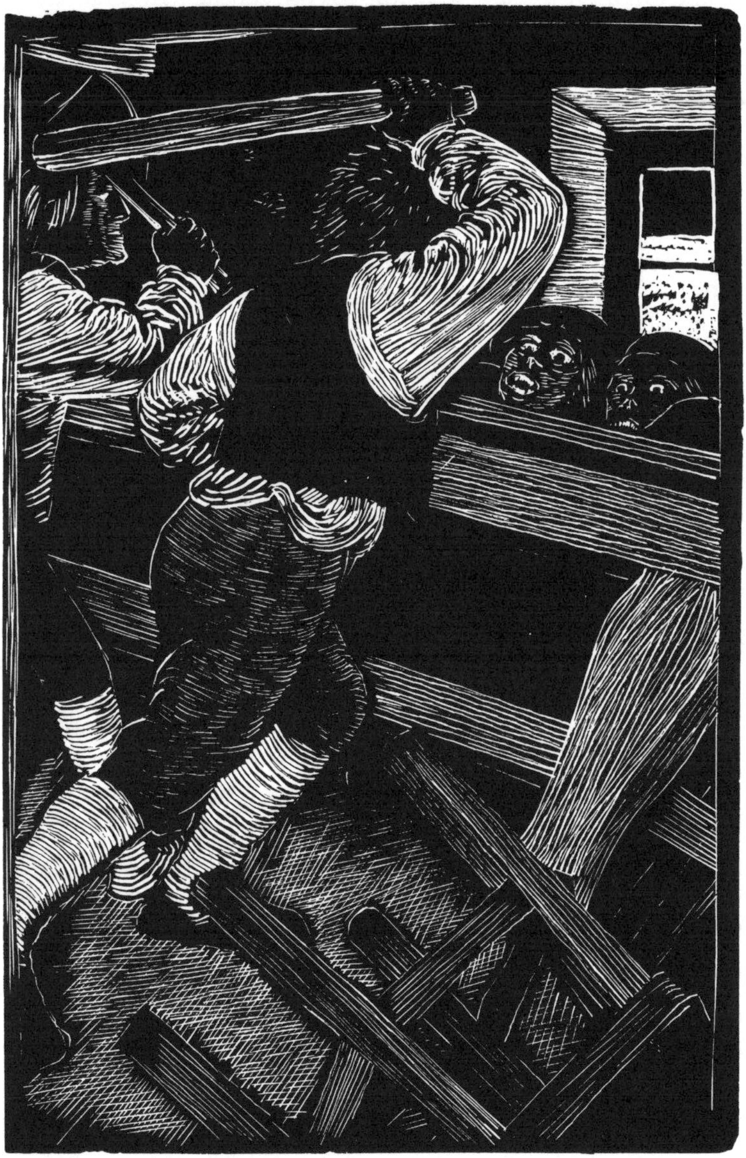

room, and despite the moonlight outside they could scarcely make out anything at all inside, for the candle had fallen down when the table was tipped over.

Then Sejer cried, 'Where do you keep the pine-sticks?* Light a couple of them on the hearth.'

'There are some lying on the chimney-piece,' shouted the old woman.

They lit them, and the room was illuminated.

'There you see, master!' said Sejer. 'I have found them and tied them up – in a sense. If you want them tethered more securely, there's some halter-rope hanging over in the corner, I see.'

They took hold of the rope, and cut it into as many pieces as there were robbers. Then they dragged them out from behind the table one by one, bound their hands behind their backs, tied their legs together as well, and threw them in a row on the floor. Then his lordship began to ask them where they came from, where their cave was, whether there were any more of them, and so on. But he couldn't get so much as half a word out of them, although he threatened them with gruesome tortures.

Then the old robber said – not to him, but to his sons: 'Just let him do as he pleases, for he has the upper hand now. But whatever he does to us shall likewise be done to him and his family; the three at home in the hill will forget neither him nor the good people of Wannet. But now you're to keep your mouths shut until the noose opens them up again!'

This threat did them no good, for when the holiday was over Jørgen Marswine had them stretched on the rack, first the old one and then the young ones. They all held out except the youngest. He confessed all their misdeeds, as well as where their cave was. This was discovered that very same day, and there they caught the robber wife as well as two of her sons, who were hanged together with the other six. In the cave they found an enormous heap of silver and gold, and among it a ring that was known to have belonged to the gentleman whose

---

* pine-sticks: splinters of pinewood found in the marshes.

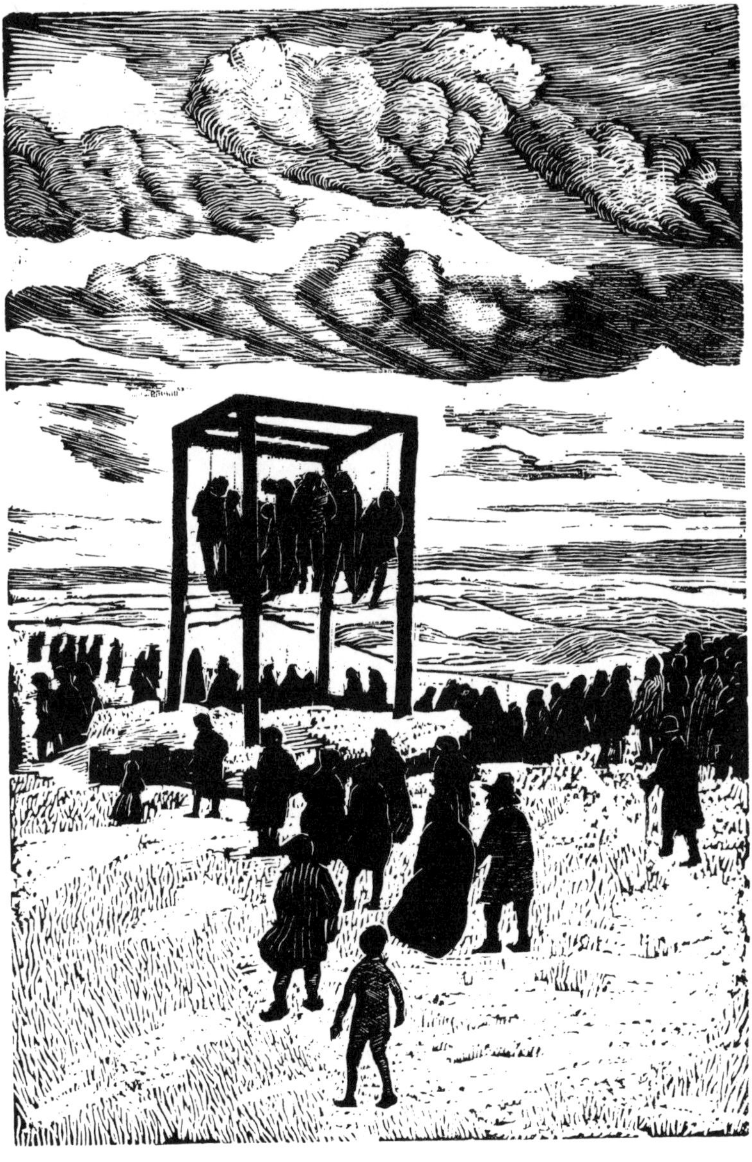

lying accusations had done so much harm to Ma-Ib's. But now this was made good again: his lordship held Sejer's and her wedding himself and kept all his promises besides, even giving them not so few of the treasures that were found in the robbers' cave. Strong-Sejer (as he was nicknamed afterwards) lived with his wife for many, many years. And all their children, and their children's children, retained the nickname. But by now it has probably died out, together with the strong lord's noble name and all his family.

But the festival eve I have just told you about ended happily – at Aunsbjerg, though most of all in Wannet.

NOTES

THE DIARY OF A PARISH CLERK

1 *he snuffed out the candle*: an old superstition, according to which someone in the house will die if the candle is snuffed out on New Year's Eve.
2 *agamus gratias!*: let us give thanks!
3 *Cornelius*: Cornelius Nepos, Roman historian c. 100 B.C. His biographies of famous men were used for elementary instruction in Latin.
4 *Amen in nomine Jesu!*: Amen, in the name of Jesus!
5 *mi fili! mi fili! otium est pulvinar diaboli!*: my son, my son! Leisure is the pillow of the Devil!
6 *die St. Martini*: Martinmas, November 11th.
7 *vellem hunc esse filium meum!*: would that this were my son!
8 *habeat!*: serve him right!
9 *Calendis Januar*: January 1st.
10 *Proh dolor! væ me miserum!*: Alas, what sorrow! Oh, how unhappy I am!
11 *fregisti cor meum*: you have broken my heart.
12 *pater! in manus tuas committo spiritum meum!*: Father! into Thy hands I commend my spirit!
13 *Seras dat poenas turpi poenitentia*: his repentance comes too late.
14 *Pridie iduum Januarii MDCCIX*: the day before January 13th.
15 *Tuticanus*: one of Ovid's friends in Rome to whom he wrote two poems in letter form while exiled to Tomis on the Black Sea.
16 *Eheu! Mortuus est!*: Alas, he is dead!
17 *Idibus Januarii*: January 13th.
18 *XVIII Calend. Febr.*: January 15th, the eighteenth day before February 1st.
19 *sing at people's doors in Viborg*: grammar-school boys used often to earn their keep in this way.

20 *Valete plurimum! vendidi liberatum*: Farewell to all! I have sold my freedom.
21 *ars amoris* (The Art of love) and *remedium amoris* (The Cure for Love): titles of two works by the Roman poet Ovid, author of *Metamorphoses*.
22 *Miss Sophie*: This character is based on the historical personage, Marie Grubbe (c. 1643–1718), a noblewoman and daughter of Erik Grubbe of Thiele. Her life story has been a source of inspiration to many Danish poets.
23 *You accept bribes*: a common hunting expression for allowing the game to escape.
24 *L'école du Monde*: The Universal Teacher, a textbook on etiquette from 1694 by the French writer Eustache le Noble.
25 *Grand Richard*: an especially fine sort of apple.
26 *J'ai froid*: I'm cold.
27 *Comment!*: What was that!
28 *Un peu, mademoiselle*: A little, Miss,
29 *Tenez, Martin! arrestez-vous!*: Wait, Martin, stop!
30 *Tartar prince*: the title character in the sentimental novel *Zingis, histoire Tartare* from 1711 by Mlle. de la Roche-Guilhem.
31 *Point de tout*: Not at all.
32 *Valet-de-chambre*: valet.
33 *ah, malheureux que je suis!*: alas, unhappy man that I am!
34 *Ah, Mademoiselle Sophie. Adieu! un éternel adieu!*: Oh, Miss Sophie. Farewell! Farewell for ever!
35 *Now I know all about war*: The war referred to is the Great Nordic War between Sweden and Russia and Denmark/Norway. Denmark made peace with Sweden in 1720.
36 *Quid hoc sibi vult?*: what does this mean?
37 *stricken the people with blains*: According to contemporary sources the plague in Copenhagen in 1711 killed about 23,000 citizens.
38 *Lord Gyldenløve*: Ulrik Frederik Gyldenløve, a natural son of King Frederik III of Denmark, was one of the country's most influential men.
39 *Un cavalier accompli, ma fille! n'est ce pas vrai? et il vous aime, c'est trop clair?*: An accomplished gentleman, my daughter, is he not? And he loves you, isn't that quite plain?
40 *Potiphar's wife*: See *Genesis* 39.

NOTES

THE GAMEKEEPER AT AUNSBJERG

1 *'der alte Fritz'*: Frederick the Great of Prussia. See Afterword p.182.

2 *settlement villages*: villages populated by German farmers, invited in 1759 by King Frederik V of Denmark to settle in the vast and hitherto uncultivated tracts of moorland in the north of Jutland. They initiated the cultivation of the potato in Denmark.

ALAS, HOW CHANGED!

1 *Miss Flamborough*: peasant girl in Oliver Goldsmith's novel *The Vicar of Wakefield* (1766), which Blicher had translated into Danish. *Betty Bouncer*: peasant girl referred to in Oliver Goldsmith's *She Stoops to Conquer*. *Lafontaine*: the German author August Lafontaine (1758–1831), writer of popular sentimental novels. *Lotte* and *Marianne*: the heroines in respectively Goethe's *Die Leiden des jungen Werther* (1774) and the Danish author J.M. Miller's *Siegwart* (1776).

2 *'All ties between us . . . a curse on it!'*: freely quoted from the Danish poet B.S. Ingemann's drama *Løveridderen* (Knight of the Lion).

3 *'Die hübschen Mädchen die bleiben fern – o Traum der Jugend, o goldener Stern!'*: 'The lovely girls, they remain afar – O dream of youth, O golden star'. From the poem *'Lauf der Welt'* (The Way of the World) by F. Förster.

4 *'Es waren schöne Zeiten, Carlos,'*: 'Those were good times, Carlos'. Quotation from Goethe's play, *Clavigo*.

THE PASTOR OF VEJLBYE

1 The *herredsfoged* was both district sheriff and judge at the *herredsting*, or district court, and was appointed by the lord lieutenant on behalf of the king.

2 *a pair of Mohrenkopper*: blue roans with black heads, legs and tails.

3 *lay your hand on the dead* refers to an old superstition that when the murderer touches the corpse of the murdered person the wounds will start bleeding.

4 Suicides and executed criminals were usually buried in a spot where three fields join to form a T.

TARDY AWAKENING

1 '... *Die holde Sittsamkeit bey Tage.*': ' ... (She is) virtue itself in the daytime.' Quotation from a ballad by the German poet G.A. Bürger (1747–94), implying that she is quite otherwise at night.
2 *tu contra audentius ito* ... : you must fight more boldly. Quotation from Virgil's *Aeneid*.
3 '*Frantz! Frantz! Steh auf! der Morgen graut*': 'Frantz, Frantz, get up! It's getting light.' Quotation from Goethe's 'Goetz von Berlichingen mit der eisernen Hand' (1773).
4 *cortex peruviana selecta*: the Latin name for cinchona bark.

THREE FESTIVAL EVES

1 *wooden horse*: a wedge-shaped wooden plank placed on edge and resting on four legs. An instrument for inflicting punishment or torture on peasants and soldiers, which went out of use at the end of the 18th century.

AFTERWORD

Knud Sørensen

Steen Steensen Blicher was born on 11 October 1782 in the village of Vium in mid-Jutland, on the border between vast and thinly populated stretches of moorland towards the west and more fertile, arable land towards the east. He was the son of Pastor Niels Blicher and his wife Kristine Marie.

His childhood home was marked by his mother's illness. She suffered from depression, with the result that her son not only became more attached to his father but was also – during periods of excessive strain – sent to stay at the neighbouring manor at Aunsbjerg belonging to his mother's uncle, Steen de Steensen.

During the 1780s the Danish absolute monarchy embarked on a series of reforms that were totally to change both rural life and agriculture: villeinage was abolished, the transition to private ownership gathered momentum, the land was redistributed and new methods of cultivation were introduced. Like many other clergymen of the time Niels Blicher too was engaged in this work. His interest and enthusiasm greatly influenced his son, who was for periods directly involved in his father's local community work and remained actively interested in agriculture and social reform for the rest of his life.

In 1799 Blicher commenced his theological studies at the University of Copenhagen. He came from a family of clergymen, and there had never been any doubt as to his chosen profession.

Blicher's studies coincided with the breakthrough of romanticism in Danish literature. But whereas the majority of Danish writers and intellectuals found inspiration in Germany, Blicher mainly looked to English poets and writers. His first contribution to literature was a highly regarded translation of Ossian's poems, published in two volumes in respectively 1807 and 1809.

Blicher completed his studies in the autumn of 1809 and was appointed grammar-school master in Randers, the east-Jutland town where he himself had gone to school. In 1810 he married his uncle's seventeen-year-old widow, Ernestine Juliane, who brought considerable capital into the marriage.

From 1811 to 1819 he administered the farm at his father's parsonage. The latter was then the incumbent of Randlev in south-east Jutland, and it was here Blicher began to write in earnest. His debut in 1814, with *Poems. Part I*, won him instant recognition as a poet.

These were difficult years. Denmark was at war with England on the French side 1807–14, and the ensuing inflation resulted in 1813 in state bankruptcy with a subsequent crisis especially in agriculture. During these critical years much private capital – including Blicher's – turned into debt, and he was obliged to apply for a benefice. From 1819–26 he was the pastor of Thorning, a parish neighbouring on that of Vium, and from 1826 until shortly before his death he was the pastor of Spentrup, north of Randers.

On the map of the Jutland peninsula the three important localities in Blicher's life – Vium/Thorning, Randlev and Spentrup – form a triangle with sides measuring 40–50 miles, and within or near this triangle are to be found most of the places he mentions in his fiction.

THE STORIES

Blicher was forty-one when, in February 1824, he published his first attempt to tell a story in prose. Until then he had been recognized as a poet, and the short story was not yet accepted as a genre in Danish literary circles; but he was short of money and had agreed to supply material for a magazine entitled Readers' Fruits, designed for the literate middle classes and the increasing number of readers in rural districts following upon the Primary Education Act of 1814. It was mainly entertaining and seldom featured anything of literary merit.

'Fragments from the Diary of a Parish Clerk' was the first result of Blicher's endeavours, and chiefly responsible for the year 1824 becoming famous in retrospect for the breakthrough of Danish prose.

Blicher may possibly have got the idea for the title and genre from a story translated from the English and subtitled "Extracts from the Diary of a Poor English Country Parson"; this had been published a couple of years previously, without mention of the author's name, in a volume of Readers' Fruits to which Blicher had contributed some poems. Precisely the diary form, told in the first person, was ideal for Blicher the *poet*, who was yet to become the *narrator*; here he was able to leave his readers to connect up the snatches of narrative to form a plot.

When the story was collected in book form nine years later Blicher made several changes and abbreviated the title to *'The Diary of a Parish Clerk'*. It is the latter edition from 1833 that has been used in this selection.

Blicher partially modelled his heroine on an authentic person, the noblewoman Marie Grubbe, 1640–1718, of Thiele Manor. Her life took a socially downhill course and was known to Blicher from older sources. He has likewise known Thiele Manor between Viborg and Randers, where his father had been a private tutor.

But Blicher was not interested in historical authenticity; he created his own chief female protagonist, Miss Sophie, and transferred the action to 1708–1753, during which period the narrator, Morten Vinge, son of the parish clerk from Føulum, writes his diary. Denmark's war against Sweden on the side of Russia 1709–20 influences Morten Vinge's fate.

The Gamekeeper at Aunsbjerg from 1839 is based on Blicher's childhood experiences during his more or less enforced stays at the manor. Built on two factual though entirely disconnected events – the execution of a servant for killing his sweetheart and the death of a gamekeeper, one Vilhelm Johansen, who had been thrown from his horse – the plot itself is nevertheless purely fictitious.

Though the story refers to the gamekeeper as Vilhelm, the reader is immediately informed that he was in fact French. He had come to Denmark as orderly for a Danish general who had been serving under the French flag during the Seven Years' War (in which Prussia and England were fighting France and her allies) when Frederick the Great of Prussia routed the French at Rossbach, Thuringia (1757). At the end of the story, after his death, his full name, Guillaume de Martonniere, is revealed, while the existence of some letters that might possibly throw light on his previous life is hinted at.

Alas, How Changed! was initially published in the journal Northern Lights, of which Blicher was then co-editor. The story was printed in October 1828 and signed 'P.Sp.'.

'P.Sp.' stands for *Peer Spillemand* (Peer the Fiddler) – a pseudonym Blicher adopted when he wished to bring the more jovial, satirical and cynical side of his personality to bear. He even has Peer criticize some of Steen Steensen Blicher's proposals for reforming society!

The story was written at a time when Blicher was somewhat despondent and had a fellow feeling for the pastor he describes – the one-time *bel esprit* who, like Blicher himself, 'lived in a quiet, tucked-away spot in the north of Jutland'. This he intimates when the narrator asks his old friend how many children he has. 'One for each finger', he replies, expressing how difficult it was to keep them in clothes, while 'to send any of them away to study would be quite out of the question.'

Ten children! That was what Blicher himself was responsible for at the time the story was written.

The Hosier and His Daughter, published in Northern Lights in January 1829, is still – like *The Diary of a Parish Clerk* – one of Blicher's most popular stories. However different they may be, both embrace a conflict between love and the social order and reveal a fundamentally tragic view of life. But whereas the latter is set in the past, the former is set in Blicher's own time among the farming community he knew and understood so well. In the surrounding moorlands a home knitting industry chiefly devoted to stockings had sprung up, and many such travelling 'hosiers' made a considerable income from selling their wares in Copenhagen or Hamburg.

The story is an example of the poetic realism wherein Blicher's especial strength lies; brief lyrical descriptions of the moorland scenery contrast starkly with human trouble and suffering and lend the story its special character – its balance and perspective.

The Pastor of Vejlbye was printed in Northern Lights in May 1829, subtitled 'A Crime Story'.

With the exception of an important appendix it is again written in diary form and based on an authentic event. In 1626 Pastor Søren Qvist of Vejlbye near Grenå was sentenced to death on the basis of the circumstantial evidence for having killed his coachman, Jesper Hovgaard, in 1607. After his execution one of his sons bored deeper into the case, and during the course of a new trial in 1634 it came to light that the chief witness and one other had committed perjury. Both were sentenced to death.

Out of this authentic account Blicher creates a tragedy – unusually compelling because, unlike its historical model, he makes the pastor confess to a crime for which he is wrongfully accused. Psychologically speaking, it is Søren Qvist's belief in the social order, and first and foremost in the God he serves, that makes it impossible for him *not* to submit to the charge and the alleged proof. It must have been so, otherwise the almighty God would have intervened.

Some weighty evidence has been produced to the effect that, via a summary in *Famous Cases of Circumstantial Evidence* from 1874 by the American S.M. Philips, *The Pastor of Vejlbye* gave Mark Twain the idea for some of the episodes in *Tom Sawyer, Detective*, first published in Harper's Magazine in 1896.

*

Tardy Awakening (Northern Lights, March 1828), like *The Diary of a Parish Clerk*, is characterized by the ambivalence between the narrator's voice and the author's own standpoint. Superficially a condemnatory description of double adultery, but below the surface a description of a bigoted, closed society in which inquisitive outrage covers over envy and jealousy, the story shocked Blicher's contemporaries. Particularly the sections not related by the storyteller, consisting of "documentary" letters from Elise to her lover and portraying a woman who has the courage to live out her feelings, were difficult to stomach at the time.

Three Festival Eves is one of Blicher's late stories, printed for the first time in a Danish popular almanac for 1841. It strikingly conveys a change in Blicher's own conception of himself as writer and 'social critic'.

Whereas in the much earlier story *The Hosier and His Daughter* Blicher clearly addresses the educated reader, telling him or her *about* the countryside and the peasantry who inhabit it before getting round to the story itself, in *Three Festival Eves* Blicher presumes that the reader knows the milieu, and narrates the story from the peasants' point of view, employing their traditional narrative form. He has become the writer who writes about and for the people.

Blicher sets the story in a past speckled with villeins and bands of outlaws, but his motive for doing so was extremely topical. From 1836 onwards Blicher was busy working for a federation between Denmark, Sweden and Norway, for a free constitution and for general armament – of the entire population. Its partial aim was to strengthen Denmark in relation to Germany, whom Blicher then regarded as a threat, and whose national turmoil subsequently led to the so-called Three Years' War of 1848–50, in which an attempt by Schleswig-Holstein to detach itself from Denmark was supported by Prussia and other German states. Whereas Blicher had hitherto regarded the absolute monarchy as the pillar of society, he now placed all future hope in the people; it is Strong Sejer, the representative of the people, who displays strength and drive and becomes the saviour of society.

Blicher is not only regarded as Denmark's first important short-story writer, but also as the writer who widened the literary, and thereby also the general conception of Denmark to include the Jutland countryside and its people. He will also go down in Danish history as having helped to generate the national will that led to the bloodless revolution of 1848 and a free constitution the following year.

He himself never came to experience the fulfilment of his political dreams. He died in Spentrup on 26 March 1848.

BIOGRAPHICAL NOTES

Povl Christensen (1909–1977) was born in Copenhagen, where he studied at the Royal Academy of Fine Arts. After his debut in 1929 he exhibited in many European countries and the USA. His work is represented in the most important Nordic art museums and in the Museum of Modern Art, New York. He illustrated several literary classics, including Andersen's fairy tales, Goethe's *Faust* and, not least, Blicher's short stories, and was awarded numerous prizes.

Paula Hostrup-Jessen was born 1930 in London, where she studied medicine. Since moving to Denmark in 1963, she has studied philosophy and worked as a freelance translator. Several of her translations of Danish classics have appeared in Britain and the USA. In 1990 she was awarded the Danish Writers Association's prize for literary translation, not least for her translations of the contemporary Danish poet-philosopher Villy Sørensen. In 1996 she was awarded the Blicher Prize.

Knud Sørensen was born 1928 in Hjørring, Jutland. After completing his education he practised as a chartered surveyor on the Limfjord island of Mors until 1980. Since 1961 he has published many collections of poetry and short stories, mostly featuring local farming communities, as well as essays and a biography of Steen Steensen Blicher. He has also written for both theatre and TV, and been awarded several literary prizes, including the Blicher Prize for 1994.